CHEATER, CHEATER

CHEATER, CHEATER

ELIZABETH LEVY

SCHOLASTIC INC.
New York Toronto London Auckland Sydney

No part of this publication may be reproduced in whole or in part, or stored in a retrieval system, or transmitted in any form or by any means, electronic, mechanical, photocopying, recording, or otherwise, without written permission of the publisher. For information regarding permission, write to Scholastic Inc., 555 Broadway, New York, NY 10012.

ISBN 0-590-45866-3

12 11 10 9 8 7 6 5 4 3 2 1   12   4 5 6 7 8 9/9

Printed in the U.S.A.   40

To the great teachers who love
their students and hate cheating

CHEATER,
CHEATER

1

"Birthday Alert! Birthday Alert!" The words were written in purple ink on the front of an envelope addressed to "Lucy Lovello — A Jolly Good Fellow." Even without glancing at the return address, Lucy knew she was holding Melanie Long's birthday invitation in her hand. At least Melanie hadn't rhymed her name with Jell-O.

Lucy turned the envelope over. The back of the envelope had been stamped with the words "Life before Death — Why Wait?" Pure Melanie. Underneath there was a birthday cake sticker — just in case anybody might have any doubts about what might be inside.

Melanie had been talking about turning thirteen ever since her last big birthday, when she was ten and "double digits," as Melanie had insisted on calling the big event. The great thing about Melanie was that she enjoyed other people's birthdays as much as her own. She gave great presents. When Lucy had turned thirteen over the summer, Melanie had sent her a stained-glass unicorn. It hung in Lucy's window catching the light.

Lucy pulled out the invitation, saw the bowling pins and groaned. *Bowling!* Lucy loved almost all sports except bowling. Lucy knew the party would still be fun. Almost anything with Melanie was fun.

She flipped open the card. School hadn't even started, but Sherwood Middle School in Indianapolis had better not schedule anything that might interfere with Melanie's birthday.

Then Lucy saw the words "Couples Only!"

"What?!" exclaimed Lucy.

Her mother came running into the room. "What's wrong?" she asked.

Lucy shook her head. "Nothing," she mumbled. Lucy's mother had a tendency to worry too much. She wrote a column on health issues for the local paper. Most of the time, she did her writing at home. Someday Lucy was sure her mother would write something like "hangnails can be fatal." Or more likely an article that explained why turning thirteen could be dangerous to your health.

Lucy didn't want to talk to her mother about Melanie's invitation — certainly not until she talked to Melanie herself.

"You look upset about something, honey," said her mother. "What is it? Of course, who could blame you? I know that going to a big school has you anxious — new teachers, a jump in your courses."

"Mom, I'm not upset," said Lucy, barely able to stop a half smile. Her mother got so many things wrong. Starting middle school wasn't the problem. Elementary school had begun to feel too small.

No, school wasn't the problem. Having to invite a boy to Melanie's party — now that ranked right up there as a problem.

It wasn't that Lucy was ugly. Lucy looked like a model for a "Hoosier," a kid straight from Indiana, "America's heartland," with long straight hair and more freckles than anybody could count. She had a thin face with a pointed chin, and wide-apart blue eyes. Her eyes were set deep in her face. Her father said her eyes gave her character, and she liked that word.

"I've got to make a phone call," Lucy said to her mother. "Private, okay?"

Lucy's mother nodded. She had written a column on a teenager's need for privacy. "I can take a hint," she said.

Lucy felt a pang of guilt. "Mom, it's not a big deal. I just got Melanie's birthday invitation. It's a *bowling* party."

"Oh, no wonder you're upset," said Lucy's mother, patting her on the back. "Don't worry. You're not that bad a bowler. You'll be fine."

"Thanks, Mom," said Lucy. She smiled. She couldn't believe that her mom would buy the idea that Lucy was worried about her bowling.

"You just don't worry about it," said her mom. "I'll leave you alone to call Melanie — but you tell that ol' Melanie that you're going to bowl nothing but strikeouts."

"Strikes, Ma," said Lucy.

"That was a joke," said her mother, who could actually be pretty funny sometimes.

Lucy punched in Melanie's number. Melanie answered the phone practically before it rang. "Hold on," she said breathlessly. "I'm on the other line." Only Melanie could make call waiting into an adventure.

Melanie's voice had a breathless, little-girl quality to it that masked the fact that she had a brain like a steel trap and an even better sense of humor.

"So what's with this 'couples only'!" Lucy demanded.

Melanie giggled. "I thought my mom was going to kill me when she found out I wrote that."

"I feel like killing you, too," sighed Lucy.

"I think it sounds grown up," said Melanie. "See, I didn't want to just invite people I knew to my birthday party. But I couldn't wait to send out my invitations until school starts. This isn't going to be a small party, you know. I'm turning thirteen."

"Why didn't you just rent the Hoosier Dome and be done with it."

"You know, some day . . ." dreamed Melanie.

"Melanie," warned Lucy. "It's a joke. The Hoosier Dome is taken — I don't think even you are going to need to seat 18,000 for your birthday."

"You're right," admitted Melanie. "Maybe Market Street Arena, where the Indianapolis Pacers play basketball. Anyhow, I love the idea of having a couples-only party. And we've got a great prize for the couple with the highest score. It's so neat. I figure bowling will give people something to do. And this way, people like you without a boyfriend — you'll probably invite somebody new, and I'll get to meet new kids from school."

"What do you mean, people like me without a boyfriend? What about people like you? You don't have a boyfriend, either."

"Dustin," said Melanie. "I've invited Dustin. We decided we're a couple."

Dustin Pappas was as much Lucy's friend as Melanie's. The three of them had been going to school together since kindergarten. Dustin was not as obnoxious as most boys. "Excuse me," Lucy exclaimed. "You invited Dustin to be your date to your birthday party? You've never dated Dustin!"

"I decided it would be good to go into Sherwood being able to tell people that I had a boyfriend. Dustin said that he didn't mind, either."

"I can't believe you didn't tell me," said Lucy.

Melanie paused. "Well, I only just got off the phone settling it with Dustin when you called," she admitted.

"This sounds like a great romance," muttered Lucy. "So who am I supposed to go with?"

"Ask anybody, but be sure to make him cute," said Melanie with a cackle. "It would be great if it were somebody new."

Lucy groaned. "Right, just go up to some stranger on the first day of class and say, 'hey, want to go to a couples-only party with me?' "

"Yeah," said Melanie, taking her seriously. "That sounds cool."

Lucy bit her lip. She looked at the couples only scrawled on the bottom in Melanie's messy handwriting. "Melanie," she sighed. "Only you could make the first day of school more complicated than it was already."

"I aim to please," said Melanie cheerfully.

2

Lucy's old elementary school building had been built twenty years ago. Sherwood Middle School was only five years old and felt like a palace compared to the cracked linoleum of the old school. It had carpeted hallways with skylights letting in sunshine from above. There was even a vending machine selling juice in one of the hallways, available to all students. The only vending machine in elementary school had been in the teachers' room, and strictly off limits to kids.

Dustin came up to Lucy after orientation. "I'm so glad to see a familiar face," he said. He was wearing a short-sleeved shirt with flapping sleeves.

Lucy wondered if Dustin had decided that the shirt made him look grown up. The shirt had wide stripes in red and blue.

"I hear you and Melanie are a couple now," she teased.

Dustin looked uncomfortable. "Where did you hear that?" he asked.

"Melanie," Lucy answered. "She said you're going to be her date for her birthday party. With Melanie, that's equivalent to being engaged."

Dustin gave Lucy a dirty look, and she realized that she was going too far.

She searched for a way to change the subject. They had been given computer printouts of their class schedules and Lucy buried her head in the schedule to cover up both hers and Dustin's embarrassment. "Uh-oh, we've got Mr. Vega for science," she whispered to Dustin.

"Why uh-oh?" asked Dustin.

"I heard about him from my cousin Steven," said Lucy. "He's supposed to be the hardest teacher in the school."

"Hey, there you are!" shouted Melanie. "I've been looking for you two for ages. What are you whispering about?" Melanie looked great. She wore her black hair in a short layered cut, and the red glasses that had practically become her trademark since fourth grade. Red was Melanie's favorite color. She was wearing a red miniskirt with red tights and a red Sherwood School sweatshirt.

"Dustin what are you doing dressed up as a flag?" Melanie asked.

Dustin blushed. "I picked out this shirt special for the first day of school," he said.

"It's cool," said Melanie.

Lucy thought the shirt made Dustin look a little dorky. She wondered whether that's what happens when you're a couple. You start lying.

"So, Lucy," asked Melanie, "have you figured out who to invite to my party?"

"Melanie, we've been in school for exactly one hour. I don't think your party is top priority. I'm still trying to figure out my schedule."

Melanie grabbed Lucy's arm. "Do you know who that is?" she whispered. "It's Joey Rich."

"Who's Joey Rich?"

"He's the son of one of the owners of the Indianapolis Pacers, that's all," said Dustin. "I'm surprised he's not in private school."

"How did you both know who he is?" Lucy asked, truly mystified.

"Everyone knows," said Melanie, nudging Dustin, immediately making Lucy feel like the third wheel.

"Everybody doesn't know," protested Lucy. "I'm somebody, and I never heard of the guy. What is there, a *People* magazine for teenagers in Indianapolis?"

"It was in the paper that he was coming to public school. I read that he was going to be in our class," said Melanie. "His father's on the school board, and there was a lot of flack because he used to go to a private school."

The boy, Joey, was dressed in a shirt almost identical to Dustin's. Lucy wondered whether somewhere there was an invisible seventh-grade uniform for boys. Joey had red hair and nearly as many freckles as Lucy.

He saw their little group staring at him, and walked toward them purposefully. There was nothing bashful or awkward about him.

Lucy smiled at him, embarrassed that her friends had made him into a celebrity.

"Hi," he said. "Do I know you?"

Lucy blushed, feeling it had been a stupid thing to smile at him as if she knew him. Maybe he thought that girls at this new school were going to be throwing themselves at his feet.

"I don't think so," admitted Lucy. "I just smiled because you looked a little lost."

Melanie giggled and nudged her with her elbow. Lucy wished that Melanie would just quit it. She gave Melanie a dirty look.

"I am lost," admitted Joey. "I'm looking for Mr. Vega's science class. Do you know where it is?"

"We're heading there, too," said Lucy. "I was just telling my friends that my cousin told me he's one of the toughest graders in school. I'm Lucy Lovello, by the way."

"Joey Rich," said Joey, sticking out his hand. Lucy had to awkwardly shift her notebook from one hand to the other. She wasn't used to shaking hands with kids. It seemed strangely formal, almost as if Joey was a politician.

"These are my friends, Melanie and Dustin," said Lucy. "We went to Como Park Elementary together."

Joey screwed his face up. "Just my luck," he muttered.

"What, that you met three kids from Como?" said Lucy. "Thanks a bunch."

Joey laughed. "No, I meant what you said about Mr. Vega. Science is my worst subject."

"Me, too," said Melanie. Lucy stared at her. Melanie was a whiz at math and science. "I'm so worried. Junior high is the pits."

Joey nodded and the four of them headed off to find Mr. Vega's class. Lucy wondered what was getting into Melanie. Melanie never found school the pits. She was too good at it to ever worry. Dustin trailed along after Melanie.

Lucy shook her head. "Being part of a couple,

I think that must be the pits," she muttered.

"What did you say?" Dustin asked.

"Nothing," said Lucy. She didn't want to repeat what she had said, because she wasn't sure
whether she believed it or not.

3

Mr. Vega had the words "Chaos" and "Order" written on the board. He was a tall man, with a large face and acne scars on his cheeks. He wore a suit with a red tie, and was dressed much more formally than any of the other teachers Lucy had seen in the halls.

He asked the students to take a seat anywhere. Lucy took a seat by the window. Dustin sat next to Lucy, and Joey sat behind her. A tall girl whom Lucy didn't know grabbed the seat in front of her, just as Melanie was about to sit down. Melanie took her books and sat in the back. The tall girl turned around.

"Can you see over me?" she asked.

"I'm not a shrimp," said Lucy. She was almost as tall as the girl in front of her. Lucy smiled. She hadn't meant to sound unfriendly.

The girl shrugged.

Just then Joey tapped her on the shoulder. "You chose the right side," he whispered.

"What do you mean?" Lucy whispered back. She had chosen the side closest to the windows because she always felt slightly claustrophobic in any closed room.

"I like chaos," said Joey with a grin, pointing to the chalkboard. They had taken seats on the "Chaos" side.

Mr. Vega read the class list. "Lindsay Levinson." The girl in front of Lucy raised her hand.

"Lucille Lovello." Lucy raised her hand. Lindsay giggled, as did a boy in the back of the room. Ever since kindergarten Lucy had had to endure jokes about her name. "Lucy Loves Jell-O — I love Lucy." It was no fun to have the same name as a dead comedienne.

Mr. Vega took a pointer and rapped on the board.

"Class, which do you think I prefer — chaos or order?"

Lucy raised her hand. "Order," she said.

Mr. Vega frowned. "That's the simplistic answer," he said.

"I told you I had the right answer," Joey whispered into Lucy's ear. He raised his hand.

"Yes, sir," said Mr. Vega.

"I think you like chaos, Mr. Vega. I think chaos is more interesting."

Mr. Vega rapped his pointer against the board. "Define 'chaos.'"

Joey raised his hand. "A big mess — like the first day of school."

Somebody right in back of them snickered, but Mr. Vega didn't look amused. "You are in science class, Mr. . . ." he paused. "Your name, sir?"

"Joey Rich," said Joey.

"I make the jokes in this class," said Mr. Vega sharply. "You will discover that there is nothing funny about chaos."

Lucy raised her hand. "I don't think Joey was trying to make a joke," she said. "You asked him a question, and he got it right. I was the one who got it wrong."

There was another giggle from the back of the class.

"Do you think that science is a debating society?" demanded Mr. Vega. Lucy felt herself blush, but she was going to hold her ground.

"Yes," she said. "I think that scientific principles are open to debate." A boy in the back of the class snickered loudly.

"Young lady, what is your name again?"

"Lucy Lovello," Lucy answered.

There was another cackle from the back of the room.

Mr. Vega banged his pointer against the board. Then he pointed it in the direction of the boy who snickered.

"Your name, sir," he demanded.

"Albert Barber," said the boy. Lucy turned around to look at the snickerer. He was tall — almost as tall as Mr. Vega — but skinny.

"Well, Mr. Barber, chaos is nothing to laugh at. Chaos is one of the laws of the universe that you will study in this class.

"Behind the most confusing-looking formulas are simple experiments. In this class, you will learn by doing — not by memorizing — and the symbols of science will become as familiar to you as any word in the English language." Mr. Vega quickly scribbled on the board:

$$KE = \frac{1}{2}mv^2$$

Melanie raised her hand. "KE stands for kinetic energy."

Joey groaned.

"Very good," said Mr. Vega. "Can you decipher the formula?"

Melanie shook her head. "I'm not sure, but I know 'v' probably stands for velocity and 'm' for momentum."

"What is your name, miss?" asked Mr. Vega.

"It's Ms. Melanie Long," said Melanie, emphasizing the word *Ms.* Someone in the back giggled at Melanie. Melanie kept her cool.

Good for Melanie, Lucy thought.

"Chaos is something you will study but I will not allow in my class," warned Mr. Vega. "You are not children to be pampered anymore. I am the only master of chaos in this classroom. I will expect you to do your work every day. There is no such thing as cramming for an exam in my class because I reserve the right to give you a quiz *without* warning at *any* time. Fully two-thirds of your *final* grade will depend on your score on these pop quizzes. If you fall behind, you will understand chaos from the inside out, as it were."

Mr. Vega laughed as if he were making a little joke. Lucy found him frightening, as if he enjoyed his superiority and power over them all.

He knocked his pointer against the formula.

"Kinetic energy — a force in physics. M will always stand for mass. V for velocity."

He turned back to the class. "Write it down, class," he warned. "I won't tell you twice."

Lucy wrote it down quickly.

4

At the end of the school day, Joey came up to Lucy. "Thanks for sticking up for me in Mr. Vega's class," he said.

"He made me mad," said Lucy. "You had the right answer. He's going to be a jerk of a teacher, I can tell."

Joey smiled. "You sure have trouble saying what you think, don't you?"

Lucy shrugged. "Are you saying I shouldn't have called him a jerk? I didn't say it to his face."

"No, he's a jerk all right. I just like the fact that you're willing to call him a jerk. Most girls wouldn't."

"I hate it when people say 'most girls' — we're not a category in a Jeopardy game, you know."

"I know," he said. "Say, look, Lucy Lovello, can I have your phone number?"

Lucy bit her lip. Nobody had ever asked her

for her phone number before in quite that way. She could remember having to memorize her phone number when she was little in case she got in trouble, but this was different — this was like a scene out of *Seventeen*, a boy asking for your phone number.

Lucy gave it to him.

"Thanks," said Joey. "In case I have any questions about the homework in Mr. Vega's class, I might call you. Is that okay?"

"Sure," said Lucy.

Melanie and Dustin found Lucy staring after Joey as he walked away.

"So what did the 'Rich boy' want?" Dustin asked.

"Don't call him that," protested Lucy.

"Why? It's his name."

"It's like calling me Love-Jell-O; it's not his fault that his name's Rich."

"Or that he is rich," added Melanie. "I never call you Lucy Jell-O."

"Right, just 'Lucy's a jolly good fellow,' " said Lucy.

"I thought you'd like that," objected Melanie. "So what did *Joey* want?"

"My phone number," giggled Lucy.

"I don't believe it," exclaimed Melanie. "You're

in school for one day and a boy asked you for your phone number. Did you ask him to my birthday party?"

"Melanie, I hardly know him. If you want him to come, invite him yourself."

Just then Lindsay, the tall girl from their science class, walked up to them. "Excuse me," she said. "But did you get the homework assignment from Mr. Vega? I wrote it down but lost it."

"I got it," said Dustin.

"Your name's Lindsay, isn't it?" asked Lucy, trying to be friendly.

"Spider," Lindsay corrected.

"Spider?" Lucy repeated.

Spider nodded. "I figure I need a *good* nickname in junior high — something I can take with me to high school. I'm gonna play basketball."

"So is Lucy," said Dustin. "Lucy's good."

"We'll see," said Spider. "One thing I love about this school. Basketball starts in the fall. Tryouts are tomorrow after school, right?" Spider seemed to be sizing Lucy up.

"I'll be there," said Lucy.

"So will I," said Spider. "Do you have a nickname?"

Lucy shook her head. "I didn't know I needed one."

Spider grinned, clearly feeling that she was one up. "It's not required, but a good nickname helps."

"Maybe you can call yourself 'The Freckle'? suggested Dustin.

"Thanks, but no thanks. I don't want to go through school being labeled The Freckle."

"That's why I picked Spider," said Spider. "It's got character."

Lucy nodded. "You're right." Lucy thought that Spider was a pretty neat name to have as a basketball player.

Spider took down the assignment from Dustin. She walked down the hall.

"She's cool," said Melanie. "I think I'll invite her to my birthday party."

"You don't even know her," said Lucy.

"I told you I want to invite some new kids to my party," said Melanie. "I want my party to shake things up."

"Your party definitely will," said Dustin. He didn't look very happy.

"Especially because Lucy's going to invite Joey," teased Melanie.

"I didn't say I'd do that," said Lucy.

"Yeah, but I know you're going to," said Melanie.

Lucy found herself smiling. She tried to hide it, but Melanie saw her and started giggling.

"You're really bad," said Lucy.

"Call him tonight," suggested Melanie. "Get it over with."

5

When Lucy got home from school, she was surprised to see that both her parents were home. She had thought her father was out of town. Her father sold farm equipment. In the summertime, Lucy would go on selling trips with her father. It was always hard to watch him be nice to people who turned him down. He'd talk to them, with his biggest smile on, and have to nod when people were rude and just turned their back on him.

"Nobody likes a salesman in hard times," said her father.

"How was your trip?" asked Lucy.

"Not bad," said her father. "How was the first day of school?"

"Yes, tell us," said Lucy's mother. She sounded a little anxious, as if she expected Lucy to come out with bad news.

"School was okay," said Lucy.

"Okay? That's all you're going to tell us about your first day?" asked Lucy's mother.

"Leave her alone," said Lucy's father. "She'll tell us more when she wants to. There's a Pacers game on TV tonight, so I'm cooking up some chili and we'll eat in front of the TV."

Lucy gave him a thumbs-up sign. Both her father and mother were big Indianapolis Pacers fans. Lucy knew she'd have to tell her parents that she had met the son of the Pacers' owner, Mr. Rich, but her father seemed to be giving her permission to tell them in her own good time.

She gathered up her books from the front hall. She picked up the three-ring notebook filled with such painstakingly written notes that she had actually included Mr. Vega's words — Chaos and Order — written in two columns. Her heavy history book came next, then Mr. Vega's science text with its complicated picture of an atom, and at the pinnacle a small Spanish book balanced precariously.

Up in her room, Lucy unloaded the books in reverse order. She liked order. Her room was neat.

She sat down at her desk and took out the science text first. The formulas swam in front of her eyes, not making any sense.

She doodled the name Lucy Rich in the edge of her paper. Then she quickly crossed it out, embarrassed that she would have done such a thing.

Melanie and she had always thought of themselves as different from those girls who thought of nothing but boys. Melanie prided herself on being original, and Lucy loved her determination *not* to be like everybody else. Melanie had always said boys were a waste of energy.

But now, Melanie seemed on the verge of thinking that boys were very important. Talk about waste!

In Lucy's house, her mother went around turning off lights to save money. Lucy wondered what it would be like to live in a house where the lights could be kept burning through the night — without any thought about wasting energy. Most likely Joey lived like that.

Chaos, Lucy thought. It was a force in nature. Joey said he liked chaos. Melanie had said that Lucy and Joey were made for each other.

Maybe if Lucy got enough chaos in her life, Joey would like her.

Lucy hadn't gotten much homework done when her mother called her to come downstairs to set up the TV tables in the living room. The Lovellos had a tradition. The basketball season

was the only time when they ate in front of the
TV. It didn't matter how bad a season the Indianapolis Pacers had, the Lovellos were loyal
fans. Lucy took a big bowl of chili.

"Come on, indulge me," urged Lucy's mom
during the first commercial break. "Tell me a
little more about what school was like."

"I've got a Mr. Vega for science. Steven got a
D minus in his class last year. He's got the reputation for being the toughest teacher in the
school. I think he's also the meanest. I know I'm
not gonna like him."

Her mother frowned. "I don't like you talking
that way about your teacher after just one day."

"Mom, why ask me about school if you want
me to tell you only what you want to hear?"

"You're right," said her mother. "I just think
there must have been some good parts. Weren't
there?"

"I met some new kids. Some of them were
nice."

"Like who?" asked her mom. Lucy knew it was
an innocent question, but still, it felt like prying.

"Joey Rich," Lucy blurted out. "You know, the
family that owns the Pacers."

Her father raised one eyebrow. "I'm surprised
a boy like that wouldn't be going to private
school."

"His dad's on the school board," said Lucy's mom. "Don't you remember seeing an article about it in the newspaper? I think it was very courageous of Mr. Rich to send his son to a public school."

"Courageous?" snorted Lucy's dad. "He'll probably keep his son there for a couple of months and then yank him out when all the publicity dies down."

Lucy didn't want to think about Joey being yanked out of school.

They settled down to watch the basketball game. Lucy took a second bowl of chili.

"So what's up for Melanie's birthday party this year?" asked her father.

"Don't talk to me about it," said Lucy, watching one of the Pacers make a terrific head-fake and drive for the basket.

"Lucy's upset because it's a bowling party," whispered Lucy's mother. "You know, Lucy, you could be a good bowler if you put your mind to it."

"I'd rather she stick to basketball," said Lucy's father. "That's the sport that's going to win her scholarships."

It was her parents' fantasy that someday Lucy would get a sports scholarship.

"It's *not* the bowling part," exclaimed Lucy. "I have to ask a boy!"

"What do you mean you *have* to? Who's making you?" asked her mother.

Lucy stared at the television set. "I don't want to talk about it," she mumbled. Lucy wondered why she had told her parents anything. This was one subject she didn't want their opinion on.

The Pacers were losing.

At halftime, Lucy gathered up her dishes and announced that she was going upstairs to finish her homework.

"Okay," said her dad. "I'll let you know if the Pacers pull it out."

"Dad, it's just an exhibition game," said Lucy.

"It's a game, and it's our team," said her father. "This could be our year."

Lucy's father said that every year, and every year the Pacers never even made it to the play-offs.

6

Lucy had half hoped that Joey would call her after school, but the phone never rang. When she got to school the next day, Lucy kept looking in the halls for Joey. It annoyed her that she was doing it, but she couldn't help herself. Finally she caught sight of him, talking to Albert. Albert was waving his hands in the air.

Albert looked extremely upset. He strode down the hall. Albert had a funny walk. He bounced on the balls of his feet, with long strides.

Joey saw Lucy staring at him and rolled his eyes up toward the ceiling.

Lucy took that as an invitation to walk over to him.

"What's up with Albert?" she asked.

"Albert asked to be transferred out of Mr. Vega's class," said Joey, "and he got turned down. He's sure that he's going to fail."

"It's only the second day of school," said Lucy. "Isn't it a little early to be worrying about failing?"

"Apparently not for Albert," said Joey.

"Did you know him at your other school?" Lucy asked.

Joey shook his head. "No, but I like him. He's a big basketball fan."

"So am I!" Lucy exclaimed. "I'm going to try out for the girls' team. Tryouts are this afternoon."

Lucy wished she hadn't sounded quite so — well — perky. It was as if she were trying to prove to Joey that she was a bigger fan than Albert.

But Joey grinned. Evidently, he didn't mind perky. "That's great. Maybe . . ."

Joey's voice trailed off. He sounded like he had a cold, as if he was trying to keep his voice from squeaking.

"Maybe what?" she prompted.

Joey stared down at the carpeted hall as if he had never seen carpeting before.

"I was going to ask you to an exhibition game this weekend. The Pacers are playing the Celtics on Friday night, but I wasn't sure that you liked basketball."

"Like it! My parents and I are absolutely nuts about the Pacers. We watched last night's game."

Joey scowled. "Don't talk to me about last night's game," said Joey. "The team stank."

"It's just an exhibition game. My dad was saying this could be our year. Of course, he says that every year. How do you feel about bowling?" Lucy's mouth had a life of its own.

She couldn't believe she had said that. Joey would think she was a perfect idiot.

"I like it," said Joey. "I'm just not that good at it."

"Neither am I. But will you come to a bowling party with me?" Lucy asked. "It's for Melanie's birthday. It's at the end of next week. Melanie said that there's a great prize for the couple who gets the highest score, but we don't have to win."

Lucy knew she was rambling again. Why had she blabbed that out about Melanie's stupid prize?

"I'll go," said Joey. "So we're set for basketball on Friday night, too?"

"I'll go," echoed Lucy. She couldn't believe the magic in those two little words, "I'll go." Just like that — she had solved the problem of

Melanie's party. Joey took off down the hall.

Lucy stared after him. Life couldn't possibly be this easy. She spun around and looked across the hallway for Melanie. Melanie was taking books out of her locker in between classes. Lucy ran over and grabbed her. "You won't believe it," Lucy said. "He asked me to a basketball game, and I asked him to your bowling party."

Melanie shrieked. "You have a date — two dates! So is he your boyfriend?"

"Melanie! I haven't gone out with him yet," protested Lucy, but not too strongly. Lucy was proud of herself. After all, junior high was supposed to be a time for change. Maybe having a boyfriend wasn't such a terrible idea after all.

"You're so lucky," said Melanie. "I wish I could be that popular."

Popular. Lucy couldn't believe that Melanie was using that word to describe her.

"Melanie, we were the ones who used to say that caring about being popular was for the permanently stupid."

"I think we might have been wrong about that," said Melanie. "I'm jealous — all I've got is Dustin. You've got the catch of the century."

7

At the end of the day, Lucy went to the gym to try out for basketball practice. In the locker room, Spider came up to her. "I hear you go with Joey Rich," she said.

"Spider, I don't *go* with him, and can't I call you Lindsay? Calling you Spider feels, well, weird."

"I don't like the name Lindsay. I like Spider." Spider grinned. "Well, don't expect it to mean that I'm going to treat you any differently."

"What?"

"That you've got a boyfriend who owns a basketball team."

"I don't have a boyfriend," said Lucy testily. "And it's his father who owns the basketball team. Not him."

"Whatever," said Spider.

Lucy and Spider walked together from the

locker room into the gym. Lucy saw Mr. Vega. He was dressed in a short-sleeved shirt sort of like the shirts Joey and Dustin had been wearing.

"What's he doing *here*?" Lucy whispered to Spider.

"He's the girls' basketball coach. Didn't you know that?" she asked, looking at Lucy as if she were dumb.

"No," said Lucy.

Mr. Vega blew his whistle, and everybody began to gather in front of the chalkboard on the sidelines.

He had written the two words "Chaos" and "Order" again.

Lucy groaned. "Not again," she muttered.

Mr. Vega's head snapped around. Lucy thought he would be angry, but he was smiling.

"In sports — the definition is easy," he said. "I want the other team to feel chaos, and you to feel order — teamwork. I want a team that's made up of *unselfish* players. And that requires what?" He paused.

Lucy raised her hand. "Looking for who's open," she said.

Mr. Vega smiled. It was the first genuine smile Lucy had seen on his face. Apparently he hadn't expected anyone to answer his question. "It requires keeping your eyes open all the time — it means pass — pass — pass — I want almost no dribbling. Is that clear? It doesn't mean showboating. Has anybody ever heard the saying that the only thing in basketball that counts is the last two minutes?"

Spider raised her hand.

"Do you believe that?" Mr. Vega asked.

Spider started to say yes. Lucy could see her thinking over her answer.

"Uh, I don't think so," said Spider. "People like to think that — but the first basket counts as much as the second or the last."

Mr. Vega smiled again. "What's your name?"

"Spider," said Spider confidently.

"You're in my science class, aren't you?" he asked. "You're Lindsay Levinson."

"Spider's my nickname — for basketball."

Mr. Vega nodded. "Well, you gave a smart answer, Spider, a very smart answer."

Lucy stared at him. She had expected him to tell Spider that her nickname was inappropriate.

Spider looked a little cocky, and *very* smug.

"Now let's see if you can give me some answers on the basketball court where it counts." He tossed the ball to Spider.

Mr. Vega quickly divided the group into teams. Spider and Lucy were on the same team.

Spider got the ball. She drove toward the basket, but her defender stuck with her.

Lucy was wide open. She waved her arms. Spider stuck an elbow into the stomach of the girl who was trying to guard her and pushed toward the basket.

The girl stumbled backward, and Spider quickly pivoted and passed the ball to Lucy.

Mr. Vega blew his whistle.

"Lucy was open before. Why didn't you pass to her then?"

"Everyone would have looked for her," said Spider. "I was being sneaky."

"Good," said Mr. Vega.

"But she fouled me," said the girl who had tried to guard Spider.

"Nobody saw it. I got away with it," said Spider with a wink toward Lucy.

Mr. Vega didn't correct her. Obviously, sneaky was good in Mr. Vega's book.

Lucy wiped the sweat from her forehead and played her best for the next hour. At the end of the tryouts, Mr. Vega made an announcement.

"Calling this session 'tryouts' was a misnomer," he said. "I have a policy for after-school sports. I think the fact that you all wanted to play means that you *should* play. That's why we start basketball much earlier than most schools.

Everyone is welcome to stay on the team. We'll have practice three times a week. As the season goes on, I'll divide you into Junior Varsity and Varsity, but right now, I want you all to enjoy yourselves."

This was a very different Mr. Vega from the one in science class, and Lucy liked this one a lot more.

"Girls' basketball is where it's at!" Lucy exclaimed.

Spider gave her a high five.

8

All that week, Lucy tried to act cool in front of Joey. She tried to pretend that going on a date was no big deal. The truth was she was very nervous.

By Friday, she would have had to describe herself as a basket case. Early Friday evening, she'd tried on six different outfits before deciding on a red shirt, black jeans, and black cowboy boots. After trying on the outfit once more, she called Melanie, and Melanie said that the cowboy boots were definitely the right choice.

When she came downstairs, her parents were both staring out the window.

"Please," begged Lucy. "What if he sees you?"

Her mother moved away from the window. "You look very nice," she said.

"Do you think I should have worn a skirt?" Lucy asked, even though she hated skirts.

"I think you look fine," said Lucy's mother. She straightened Lucy's bangs. "A first date can be very stressful," she said sympathetically.

"For me or you?" asked Lucy. Her mother laughed. Her mother had a great laugh. "We did say that you could date once you got into junior high. I just didn't expect it to happen right away."

"Mom, I know people who were dating in the fifth grade," said Lucy. She was jittery enough herself. She didn't need her parents to be tense.

"You *won't* believe this," said Lucy's father. He motioned Lucy and her mother over to the window. A white limousine had pulled up in front of the house. The windows of the limousine were tinted so that no one could see inside.

"I think picking you up in a limousine is a little much," said Lucy's father.

Lucy swallowed hard.

The doorbell rang. Joey looked a little anxious, too. He was dressed in pressed chinos and a sweater. Lucy introduced him to her parents.

"We're big Pacers fans," gushed Lucy's mother. Lucy wished her mother hadn't gushed.

"Yeah, Lucy told me," mumbled Joey. "Look, we've got to be going. My dad's in the car."

"Are you sure your dad wouldn't want to

come in?" asked Lucy's father, peering out the window.

"Uh, no, sir," said Joey. "My dad likes to get to the game early."

"He probably likes to go down and give a pep talk to his players," said Lucy's mother, pretending that she didn't know Mr. Rich's reputation for bawling out his players before most games.

Joey's head bobbed up and down.

"Well, Joey, we want Lucy home an hour after the game ends," says Lucy's father. Her mother nodded.

Lucy held her breath. She was sure that her mother was going to announce that this was Lucy's first date. Instead, her mother gave her a kiss good-bye.

"He seems like such a nice boy," she whispered.

"Mom, he hardly said ten words," Lucy whispered back. "How could you tell?"

"A mother can tell," said her mother. Lucy wondered what her mother had been able to tell about Joey, except that his father had a limousine. The only time that Lucy had been in a limousine was when her great-grandmother died.

Both her parents came to the front door.

"I wish they'd stop beaming," Lucy muttered to Joey.

"They seem really nice," said Joey.

Lucy looked at him. She said the same thing to him that she had just said to her mother. "They only said ten words."

"They seem pretty low-key," said Joey.

Lucy didn't know why it annoyed her to have Joey think her parents were low-key, but it did. "You should see them cheering for the Pacers," she said. "You wouldn't call them low-key at all. In fact, they're really high-strung."

Joey didn't answer her. Just then the chauffeur jumped out and opened the door to the back seat. Lucy wanted to make a joke about whether the driver thought she and Joey were too weak to open their own door, but she thought better of it. The man was dressed in a gray uniform and was wearing white gloves.

Inside the limousine, Lucy recognized Joey's father from the times she had seen his picture in the paper. He had Joey's fair skin, but everything about him was big. His face was big. His hands were big. Even his feet were big.

He nodded at Lucy and gave her a smile. He was talking on a cellular phone.

Lucy and Joey sat on the seats that faced the

trunk. There seemed to be a mile of plush carpeting between their seats and the seat where Joey's father was sitting. If someone ever asked her what she most remembered about going on her first date, Lucy would probably reply, "the carpet." Lately, almost everywhere she went had carpeting.

Joey was fidgety. "Do you want a soda?" he asked as the car pulled away. Right next to Lucy were two heavy crystal glasses. Above the glasses was a little four-inch television.

"Is this how you travel all the time?" Lucy whispered.

Joey's father hung up the phone and immediately punched in another number. He sounded very angry at whomever he was talking to, but Joey pretended to ignore his father.

"So what'll you have? Pepsi? Diet Coke?"

Joey's father gestured impatiently for them to keep quiet. Joey lowered his voice. "What do you want to drink?" Joey's voice was lower than a whisper. He mouthed the words.

His father gave him a funny look.

"I don't need anything," Lucy whispered, but Joey poured the soda anyway.

Lucy fingered the heavy glass. The carpeting covered the toes of her cowboy boots.

Joey's father hung up the phone.

"So," he said, "Joey tells me that you're the best girl basketball player in the school."

Lucy looked at Joey. It was a lie, and Lucy knew it. They'd only had tryouts, and Joey hadn't been there. If he had, he would have taken Spider to the game.

"I'm good," said Lucy, "but I'm not the only one. I . . ."

"There," interrupted Joey's father. "Joey, did you see the way she said, 'I'm good'? That's the sign of a winner. Larry Bird used to say that all those people who said he didn't have natural talent didn't know what they were talking about."

Mr. Rich nodded his head approvingly at Lucy. "I like that. You'll make the team."

"Everybody makes our team," said Lucy. "The girls' basketball coach says that everyone who wants to play can." Lucy turned to Joey. "I scoped out the competition, though. Spider and me are the best."

"Spider and I," corrected Mr. Rich. Lucy blushed.

"Joey tells me that you two are going to a bowling party together — and there's some sort of a prize."

Lucy's eyes widened, and she stared at Joey.

She couldn't believe that Joey had told his father about the bowling prize.

"It's my best friend's birthday party," said Lucy. "I'm sure the prize is something goofy."

"Winning's never goofy," said Joey's father.

Joey nodded.

Lucy sank back on the plush seats. The seats felt weird, as if they were swallowing her up.

The limousine pulled into the underground garage beneath the arena. The driver jumped out and opened the door. Mr. Rich got out first. He strode into the Market Street Arena, glancing behind at Joey. "I'll see you up in the box," he said. "And Joey, stand up straight. Don't round your shoulders. Take some lessons from your friend there. She's got good posture."

"Your dad's sure got a lot of opinions," Lucy whispered to Joey.

Joey shrugged, rounding his shoulders even more. "Come on," he said. From the parking lot they took an elevator up to the box level. A guard smiled at Joey. Naturally, the elevator was carpeted.

Joey took Lucy into the owner's box. Lucy thought that it looked more like a living room than a place to watch basketball. In the back of the box there was a full kitchen. A half dozen covered hot trays had been placed on the countertop. Three television sets were mounted on one wall. A dozen people stood around. There were no other kids except for Joey and her.

Lucy walked to the front of the box. There were a few folding chairs set up near the window. She was walled in by thick glass. She could hear the noises from the crowd, but they were really muffled.

Joey came over to her and watched the players warming up.

"Do you want a Chinese dumpling?" he asked.

Lucy shook her head. "I want to see the action," she said.

"Mostly we watch the game on TV," said Joey. "My dad says you can study the play action much better that way."

"But we could stay home and watch it on TV," Lucy pointed out.

Joey looked hurt, and Lucy wondered if he was mad at her for not appreciating the great honor of being in the owner's box. She wanted to see the game live!

Joey went to the back of the box where the food was. Lucy followed him and took a dumpling. Chinese dumplings were *not* her idea of basketball food. "*Ummm*, delicious," said Lucy. Joey looked pleased.

Lucy wandered back to the front of the box and pressed her nose against the glass. She could hear the crowd roar as the whistle blew. The referee threw the ball up for the opening toss. The Pacers' center tipped it back to the guard. The guard looked right and tossed the ball back to the center. The center was in perfect position, right outside the three-point line. The other team was caught flatfooted. The center took a moment to collect himself and then lightly tossed the ball. It swished through the basket.

An opening three pointer. The crowd went wild. Lucy let out a loud cheer and gave Joey a high five. Joey slapped her hand tentatively as if he were embarrassed that she was showing so much enthusiasm.

Lucy glanced back. The people in the box had barely stopped talking. Joey's father came over and looked down at his players.

"Did you see that shot?" Lucy asked. "It was awesome."

"I saw it on the monitor," said Joey's father. "It's only the last two minutes that count in a basketball game."

"I don't think that's true," said Lucy. She remembered what Spider and Mr. Vega had said. "The first basket counts as much as the last."

"For a girl, you know a lot about basketball," said Mr. Rich. Lucy didn't like that "for a girl" part, but she held her tongue. She was worried that Joey would be upset if she talked back to his father.

Lucy sneaked a peek at Joey. He sat with his arms folded across his chest. Then Lucy turned her attention back to the court and watched the game. Unfortunately, after that opening three pointer, the Pacers went downhill. Well before the final two minutes, it was clear that the Indianapolis Pacers were going to lose.

Mr. Rich threw his program down on the carpet. "A bunch of losers," he muttered. "They'll hear from me tonight." He stormed out of the box.

"I still think it was a good game," Lucy said to Joey.

Joey shook his head. "We lost," he said.

"It's an exhibition game. It doesn't count," she said. "And I think they're looking great. They've really . . ."

Lucy didn't get a chance to finish her sentence. "Did I hear you say it didn't count?" interrupted Joey. His face was red.

Lucy started to get a little nervous. Joey sounded like his father.

"I think your team played well," said Lucy.

"They *lost*," snapped Joey. He put on his coat. "Come on. It's time to leave."

Lucy yawned. She had read once that yawning was a psychological response to stress. She yawned so widely that her jaw cracked and she quickly covered her mouth. She didn't need Melanie to tell her that it wasn't right to yawn in your date's face — particularly on your first date.

9

Joey didn't talk much as they took the elevator down to the parking garage. All the cars seemed to be leaving the underground garage at one time. Lucy and Joey were in the back of the limousine, stuck in underground traffic. Mr. Rich had stayed at the arena. Lucy was sure that he was going to the locker room to yell at the players.

Joey didn't sit next to Lucy. He sat backward in the jump seat. "I can't believe what you said about the game not counting," he said with his arms crossed over his chest.

He was making her mad. Joey hadn't seemed half as involved in the game as she was, and now she was being put down for not caring enough. Joey didn't look quite as cute to Lucy right now.

Joey tried to change the subject. "Isn't it neat to have a TV in a car?" he asked.

Lucy shrugged.

"What's wrong?" Joey demanded.

"You shouldn't get mad at me," said Lucy. "I'm the one who loves sports. I know what it's like to win."

"Yeah," said Joey. "Well, you'd just better hope that we win at that bowling party. What kind of prize is it?"

Lucy still couldn't believe that Joey was making such a big deal out of that prize.

"I don't know what the prize is," said Lucy.

"Don't you hope we win it?" Joey asked. His voice was softer now, a little nicer. In the dim light of the limousine, he smiled. He was definitely cuter when he smiled. He reached forward and touched Lucy's hand. "We could be a winning team. I think my dad liked you."

Lucy swallowed hard. Her hand felt clammy. She didn't know how to tell Joey that she hadn't really liked his dad.

"I was pretty rude to your dad. I'm worried that maybe he thought I talked too much."

Joey shook his head. "As we were leaving, Dad said that you've got a lot on the ball. That's a real compliment coming from my dad."

"It can't be easy having the name Rich," Lucy said. "Everybody in Indianapolis knows who your dad is."

"You don't have to feel sorry for me," said Joey. He sat back in the seat. Lucy felt as if there were acres of carpet between them. As they pulled up in front of Lucy's house, Lucy saw the venetian blind in the living room shimmy. She knew that her mother or father had been looking out.

The chauffeur opened the limousine door, and Lucy stepped out and waited for Joey. Joey walked her to the front door. "Well, 'bye," he said. "I'll see you in school on Monday."

"Okay," said Lucy. Joey turned and practically ran back to the limousine. "Thank you!" Lucy shouted to his back. Joey waved.

When Lucy went inside, the front hallway was empty, as was the living room. She put her coat away. "Come out, come out wherever you are!" she sang out.

Her parents came out of the den. "We didn't want to look overanxious," said her mom.

"I saw you at the window," said Lucy.

"Are you hungry?" Lucy's mother asked.

Lucy held her stomach. "No," she said. "There was more food than I've ever seen — salami, pastrami, Chinese dumplings. I feel like the Pillsbury Doughboy."

"So how was the Doughboy?" asked Lucy's father. "I mean Mr. Rich, not Joey."

Lucy's mother shot him a dirty look. "Len, that's not nice," she said. "I'm sure Mr. Rich is a very nice man."

"Actually, I didn't really like him," Lucy said quietly, relieved to be able to finally speak her mind. "All he cares about is winning, but he doesn't even watch the game. It was gross."

"That's what I always thought of him," said Lucy's father.

"Len," warned Lucy's mother, "Lucy went out with Joey — not with his father. Did you have fun?"

Lucy didn't know how to answer the question. She yawned. "Kind of," she said.

"Just kind of?" urged her mother.

"It was confusing," said Lucy. "I don't know. I think I've had more fun when we all go together and don't sit behind a big plate-glass window."

"But what about Joey?" asked her mother. "Didn't you like him?"

"Ma!" begged Lucy.

Lucy's mother put her hand up to her mouth.

"You're right. That's such a mother question. I take it back. You're entitled to your privacy."

Lucy went upstairs. Lucy wasn't sure it was privacy that she wanted. She wasn't at all sure *what* she wanted.

Well, at least next week, she and Joey would have a date without Mr. Rich. Next week was Melanie's birthday party, and maybe without his father, Joey would be more fun. But why was Joey making such a big deal about the prize?

Lucy had a feeling that the only way their second date was going to be a success was if they won. She wished she were a better bowler.

10

On Monday, as Lucy got to school, Joey was standing outside talking to a group of kids. He ignored Lucy.

Lucy felt herself blush. She would have liked just a little hello, a sign that there was something between them.

Melanie walked into school with Lucy. "So how come you still haven't told me that much about your date?" she asked.

"Melanie, there isn't that much to say. It was kind of fun, but . . ."

"But what?" insisted Melanie. Melanie had been pumping Lucy for the details of her date all weekend *and* on the school bus. Lucy was getting tired of it.

"I don't see you and Dustin together all the time," Lucy snapped.

"What's that got to do with anything?"

Melanie asked. "You sure got up in a grumpy mood this morning."

Spider came up to them. "I watched the Pacers on TV Friday night. It was a good game even though they lost."

Lucy was relieved to have a change of subject. "I thought they had a chance," she said. "They made some really good plays."

"Excuse me," said Melanie. "Is anybody thinking of anything except sports?"

"Not me," said Spider. "And speaking of, uh, sports, thanks for inviting me to your bowling party. Albert and I are going to win that prize."

"Albert?" asked Lucy. "That's who you invited?"

"Yeah," said Spider. "Why not? He's funny, and he's tall. There're not many boys I know who are as tall as I am."

"You'd better have a good prize, Melanie," warned Lucy. "Joey even told his father about it."

"Well, I wanted people to be excited about my party," said Melanie. She sounded a little nervous.

"You do have a prize, don't you?" Lucy asked.

"Yeah, it's one I thought was neat."

"Well, don't worry about it," said Lucy. "You're not supposed to worry on your birthday."

Melanie grinned. They walked down the hall to Mr. Vega's class. "Did you study this weekend?" Melanie asked.

"Please," said Lucy. "I didn't have time. First I was all nervous before the date — then I was nervous after. Did you study?"

Melanie shrugged.

"That means yes, doesn't it?" groaned Lucy. "I know you. You studied."

Mr. Vega came into the class.

"Good morning, class," he said. "Today we will have a pop quiz."

"You didn't tell us anything about a quiz," protested Spider.

"I told you on the first day of class that there would be pop quizzes throughout the term. Class, put away your books. This quiz will take the whole hour."

Lucy put her books down on the floor.

She almost bumped heads with Dustin. "I didn't study," she whispered. "I'm gonna flunk."

"He did warn us," said Dustin.

Lucy scowled. She sat back up and waited for the quiz. Mr. Vega handed it out face down. "Do not turn it over until I tell you to," he said.

Lucy fingered the corner of the test nervously. When Mr. Vega had given the tests to the entire class, he said, "Now."

Lucy flipped it over. She read the first paragraph. Every word seemed to have too many syllables in it.

> *Below are six basic formulas defining an important precept in physics. Name each formula and suggest a possible experiment for each one.*

"Hey," shouted Albert, "you'd have to be Einstein to do this quiz."

"Albert, one more word from you and you're out of the class," said Mr. Vega, sounding as if he wasn't kidding.

Lucy studied the rest of the exam. The formulas might as well have been written in hieroglyphics. The first chapter of their science book had given basic formulas, but Lucy had skipped that chapter because it was so boring. Mr. Vega had emphasized experiments over memorizing formulas. It wasn't fair.

Only one looked familiar: $E = MC^2$.

Thank goodness Albert had made that crack about Einstein.

Lucy wrote down Einstein's name, but then her pencil stopped. She couldn't think of anything else to write.

Dustin was scribbling on his paper. Lucy tried not to look at his test paper, but she was desperate. She kept peeking across the aisle. The next formula was $P = mv$.

P had to stand for power. Lucy wrote down the word power.

Dustin had turned his paper around so he could write with his left hand.

Lucy thought she saw the word "momentum."

"Lucy," snapped Mr. Vega. "Keep your eyes to yourself. I shouldn't have to treat you like a kindergartner. I expected that you learned *something* in elementary school."

Lucy felt her cheeks flame.

She turned away. She was so embarrassed that Mr. Vega had caught her cheating — well, she hadn't actually cheated. It wasn't her fault that her eyes had wandered. Dustin should have covered his paper.

She studied the last question.

$W = fd$.

W had to stand for work, but what did fd stand

for — florist delivery? Flunked deliberately? Lucy didn't have a clue.

Finally she wrote down:

Work equals the grade I'm going to get because I didn't study enough. D equals the grade I'd like to get. And A is out of sight and not even in the formula, but I promise to study harder in the future. And I wish the F stood for future, not flunked.

She signed her name in big letters.

Lucy Lovello

11

Mr. Vega handed back the exams the next day. "This is a sorry group of test answers. Do you students think that you're going to be coddled in this school the way you were in elementary school?"

Lucy chewed on a fingernail. Mr. Vega handed her the paper. She closed her eyes. She almost failed. She had gotten a D minus.

Dustin looked at his grade. He crumpled his paper. Mr. Vega frowned. "Dustin, you did good work on this test. There was no curve to this class — just an abyss. Don't worry about it."

"What did you get?" Lucy asked Dustin.

"C plus," said Dustin.

"I got a D minus," said Lucy. "I'm gonna flunk this course."

Dustin gave her a funny look.

"What?" demanded Lucy, feeling a little guilty.

"Did you think I cheated? I only took a tiny little peek and then I made myself look away. Honest."

"Lucy," hushed Dustin. "It's me — I'm your friend, remember? I didn't say that you cheated."

"I thought you thought that I did."

"I didn't," hissed Dustin.

"Dustin, Lucy, no talking," warned Mr. Vega as he finished passing out the tests. "Let's go over the quiz."

Mr. Vega wrote the exam questions on the board. "I didn't expect miracles, students. But the joy of science comes from asking questions. You can't know what questions to ask unless you know what you're doing. Fundamentals. Fundamentals. It's the same thing that I preach in basketball. I want everybody to breathe in for four counts, hold it for eight, and breathe out for eight."

"What for?" asked Albert.

"Because I'm going to try to teach you how to prepare your brains for work," said Mr. Vega.

Lucy took a deep breath while counting to four. She held it for eight counts and she felt as if her head was expanding, as if there were pockets of space under her eyes.

She let out her breath. Mr. Vega rapped his

pointer on the final formula. W = fd.

"Look at it — it looks like something you'd never want to learn. W = fd. It doesn't sound like English, but if you take it apart — it's the lesson of life. Work equals the applied force and the distance it is applied. I'm going to read the answer from one of the quizzes to you:

"Work equals the grade I'm going to get because I didn't study enough. D equals the grade I'd like to get. And A is out of sight and not even in the formula, but I promise to study harder in the future. I wish F stood for future, not flunked."

"I'm sorry," Lucy blurted out. "I wasn't trying to be smart-alecky. I just didn't know the answer."

Mr. Vega put down his pointer. Lucy was worried that she had infuriated him.

"I wasn't even going to give your name, Lucy. And that answer was the only reason that you *didn't* flunk."

"Teacher's pet," teased Spider.

"Lindsay, be quiet, please," said Mr. Vega. "Lucy tried to think originally — she looked at the formula and didn't let it freeze her blood — that's all that I want from you. I'm willing to bet that when I handed out the exam yesterday, half of you stopped breathing. Without oxygen to the brain, you can't work. Knowledge doesn't come from memorizing, but from breathing — remember that. You can't do any work unless you're breathing. Take a deep breath — and then apply that force. Physics isn't just a bunch of formulas. It's the very force of the universe."

Lucy waited for Melanie after Mr. Vega had dismissed the class.

"What did you get?" Lucy asked Melanie.

Melanie smiled. "A minus."

"A minus!" Lucy shrieked. "You've got to be kidding. That test was impossible."

"It was all in the first chapter," said Melanie.

"I can't believed you aced that exam," said Lucy.

"Well, it wasn't that easy. I've had a lot on my mind," said Melanie.

Lucy smiled at her. "Don't worry. Nobody can forget that your birthday party is this Saturday."

"Did you get me a present?" Melanie asked.

"Melanie, I've had your present for a month now."

Melanie grinned. She loved presents. "What's Joey getting me?" she whispered.

"I don't know," said Lucy. The truth was that Joey and she hadn't talked all that much since their one date.

"There he is, maybe you should ask him," said Melanie, nudging her. Lucy felt awkward. Joey was whispering to Albert. What if they were talking about her?

"What are you going to do, put up a metal detector in case someone comes to your party without a present?" Lucy asked Melanie, feeling a little bit mean.

Melanie stuck out her lower lip. "You don't think I'm greedy, do you?"

Lucy shook her head. "No, you give great presents," she said, thinking of the stained-glass unicorn.

Melanie looked relieved. "I'll see you later."

Lucy glanced over at Joey. She realized she'd better remind him about Melanie's party. She walked over to him.

"Hi," said Joey.

"Hi, yourself," said Lucy.

"What did I do wrong now?" Joey asked.

Lucy took a breath — held it and counted to four. Then expelled all the air. "Nothing," she said, trying to breathe normally. "How did you do on the exam?"

"I got an F," said Joey. "You're lucky to be sitting next to Dustin. I've got Albert as my seatmate. We both flunked."

"I didn't cheat," said Lucy.

Joey just raised his eyebrows. "I didn't," protested Lucy.

"I think Mr. Vega should be taken to court for cruelty to children," said Joey.

"We're not children anymore — I think that's his point," said Lucy.

"Bye, guys," shouted Albert as he broke away from their circle. "I'll see you later, Joey. I've got to practice my bowling. Spider and I are going to win the prize."

"No way," said Joey. "That prize belongs to Lucy and me."

Albert just shook his head as he bopped down the hallway.

"We are going to win, aren't we?" Joey said.

"I hope so," said Lucy.

"Hope?" teased Joey. "We've got to do more than hope. We can't let Spider and Albert win it."

"Speaking of Melanie's party — you know it's on Saturday. Did you get her a present? Melanie loves presents. It doesn't have to be big, but you should get her something."

"Melanie's really smart, isn't she?" said Joey.

Lucy felt inadequate. "Yeah, she's a brain. She's also my best friend. Maybe you could get her a book."

"Yeah, maybe," said Joey. "Well, I'll see you." He took off after Albert down the hall. Lucy followed him with her eyes. Boys were very hard to figure out. She liked it better when she didn't have to try. At least she got better grades.

12

When Lucy got home that evening, she took out the present she had bought for Melanie. It was a genuine crystal pendant that she had found at a crafts fair over the summer. The crystal was supposed to bring Melanie good luck. Lucy thought it was beautiful. She carefully wrapped the present, putting glitter stickers on the wrapping paper. Then she put it away. She was really looking forward to giving it to Melanie.

On Friday night, the night before the party, Joey called Lucy at home. "Hi," he said. "What time do you want to be at this party tomorrow?"

"Noon," said Lucy. "What time will you pick me up? Eleven-thirty? I really don't want to be late."

"Look, do you mind if I meet you there? It'll be easier."

"Easier for who?" Lucy asked.

"Hey," said Joey, softly, "don't get mad."

"I'm not," said Lucy quickly. She didn't want to have a fight. "Why can't you pick me up, though?"

"I told Albert I'd go with him," said Joey.

"I thought he was going with Spider," said Lucy.

"*She* doesn't mind that Albert's meeting her there," said Joey. "Albert's mother will give us all a ride home. And by the way, do *we* have a present for Melanie?"

"Well, I do," said Lucy. "But it's kind of personal. I thought you were going to get her a book."

"I forgot," said Joey. "Would you sign my name to your present? I mean, we're going as a couple."

"Sure," she found herself saying.

"Thanks for helping me out with the present. I'll see you at the party." Joey hung up.

Lucy stared down at the present that she had so carefully wrapped for Melanie. The present was personal. Why had she said "yes"?

Lucy took out her card. It was a silly card with a coyote on it. Lucy signed Joey's name next to hers. She liked the way the two names looked.

So what if he hadn't gotten Melanie his own present? They were a couple.

The next morning, Lucy took care dressing. She put on a big shirt that looked like a patchwork quilt. She loved the shirt. She had found it at the same crafts fair where she had found Melanie's present. She put on a pair of black tights underneath the shirt, and black shoes. She tried putting on some makeup over her freckles, but it gave her a weird, ghostly look. She washed her face again and settled for a little light-brown mascara on her pale eyelashes. Then she pulled her hair back with a velvet band and pinched her cheeks.

When she went downstairs her mother said, "You look terrific."

"Thanks. Mom, will you give me a ride over to the bowling alley? It's at the Crooked Creek Mall."

"Aren't you going with Joey?" her mother asked, sounding anxious.

"He's meeting me there," said Lucy.

Her mother looked at her. "It's fine with me that Joey's going separately," Lucy said quickly. "In fact, I was the one who suggested that we meet there." Lucy hardly ever lied. But that lie came out of her mouth before she'd even thought about it.

Her mother put her arm around Lucy. "You know, it can be very confusing being a teenager."

Lucy rolled her eyes.

"I guess I do sound a bit like one of my columns sometimes," said her mother with a laugh.

"Tell me about it," said Lucy.

"I'll give you a ride. And you do look fantastic."

"Thanks, Mom," said Lucy.

13

Lucy arrived a little late. Twenty kids had been invited and almost all of them were already there, including Joey. Melanie was in the center of it all, and Joey was right by her side. Lucy made her way up to Melanie.

"Happy birthday!" she said, giving Melanie a kiss on the cheek. Melanie was wearing a satin bowling shirt with the words "Boogie's Diner" on it.

"Where did you get the shirt?" Lucy asked her.

"Mom and Dad bought it. They saw it in a catalogue. Isn't it great?"

One of the things that Lucy liked best about Melanie was that she was not at all shy about saying it when she felt she looked good.

"We got you a present," said Joey. "Didn't we, Luce?"

Lucy didn't like the nickname "Luce." It sounded too much like loser.

"Yes," said Lucy, not correcting Joey. She handed Melanie the carefully wrapped present with the glitter star wrapping. "It looks beautiful," said Melanie. "I hope you guys have good luck. I really want you to win the prize."

"Oh, we will, won't we, Luce?" said Joey.

That was one "Luce" too many for Lucy. "It's Lucy," she said.

"Right, like in 'I Love Lucy,'" teased Joey. He smiled at her. He did have a terrific smile.

Lucy went to get her bowling shoes. Dustin was in line at the counter. "I'm a lousy bowler," he confided. "I wish Melanie had picked anything except a bowling party."

"Me, too, Dustin," said Lucy, "but it's supposed to be fun. Don't get wound up about it."

"Sure, with Melanie going on and on about the prize. You'd think it was the ten-million-dollar bowling prize," said Dustin.

Joey came and sat down next to them. "You look good," he said to Lucy. "I like that shirt. It's a winner. Just like us."

Lucy felt herself blushing. She liked the compliment and the way Joey said "us," but it was embarrassing to have him talk that way in front of Dustin.

"Yeah," said Lucy, determined not to disappoint Joey. "We're both winners."

"Hey, hey, hey, everybody relax, the master is here." Albert plopped down on the bench next to Joey. Spider came over carrying both hers and Albert's shoes.

"If you're such a master, how come you can't carry your own shoes?" complained Spider.

Spider sat down next to Lucy. "Personally, I think this couples-only stuff is for the birds."

Lucy laughed. Personally, she kind of agreed.

Melanie's mother had divided the group into teams. Joey and Lucy ended up bowling in an alley with Melanie and Dustin. Albert and Spider were in the next alley over.

"Are you ready to win?" Joey asked. They went to the rack to pick out their bowling balls. Joey picked up and put down about a dozen different balls, testing their weight carefully. Lucy picked a red one with black coloring in it, mostly because she liked its looks.

Melanie's mother blew a whistle. "It's time for Melanie to begin the birthday games!" she shouted.

Melanie took a bow, obviously loving the attention. She held the ball over her head.

"Careful you don't drop it and scramble your brains," shouted Albert.

Melanie stuck out her tongue at him.

She took another bow, and then finally faced the bowling pins. She took three steps and flung back her hand, dipping deep down like a professional. At the last moment, she took her eyes off the pins and glanced up to see if everyone was watching. Her ball ended up in the gutter. Dustin gave her a thumbs-up sign.

"Oh, well," said Melanie, "my mom told me that we couldn't win the prize anyhow."

Melanie flitted around from booth to booth, making sure that all her guests were having a good time. Lucy watched her enjoying herself.

"She's just the belle of the bowl," said Dustin.

"Dustin, that's pretty good," admitted Lucy.

"Thanks," said Dustin. "It's better than our score." Between them, Dustin and Melanie hadn't even gotten eighty points. They had by far the lowest score at the party.

Joey and Lucy were doing much better. "Lucy, it's your turn," said Joey. He handed her the ball.

Lucy looked down the alley. She remembered that her father had always told her to aim not at the lead pin, but right between the two and three and to keep her thumb up.

Lucy squinted and took three steps. Her legs were strong as she dipped down. She swung her arm and let go of the ball. It bounced so hard in the alleyway that Lucy was sure it would leave a dent.

The ball veered toward the gutter, but halfway down it curved back toward the center. It hit the pins without much power behind it. The pins collapsed onto each other, spinning on the floor. Finally only one was left standing, but before the sweeper could come down, the nine pin fell over.

"A strike?" Lucy shrieked. She couldn't believe it.

"Dumb luck," said Albert from the next alley.

Joey dashed out and caught Lucy up in a big hug.

"That's my girl," he said, loud enough for everyone to hear. Lucy's mood took a definite upswing. She absolutely loved Joey calling her "my girl." And they were winning.

Joey went next, bowling for a spare.

"Hey, Albert! How are you and Spider doing?" shouted Joey.

"We're bringing in the points — piling them on," said Spider.

Joey frowned. "Lucy, go over there and check them out. Trip Albert while you're at it."

"That's cheating," said Lucy.

"Well, do it when nobody's looking," teased Joey.

14

Lucy walked around the back of the bowling alley to the booth where Spider and Albert were playing.

"I hear you're racking up high points over there," said Spider, looking up from her scoring. Albert had just added a seven to his spare from the last frame.

"We're doing okay, but it looks like you're doing well, too," said Lucy.

"Albert's got his flaws," said Spider. "But losing isn't one of them. Whoops, got to go. It's my turn."

Spider got up and took her ball from the rack.

"Come to spy on the opposition?" Albert asked Lucy.

Lucy felt a little foolish. She watched as Spider tested her ball. Just as Spider had her hand back, getting ready to let the ball go, Lucy sneezed. It was one of those sneezes that sound like an earthquake.

Spider dropped the ball into the gutter. Albert gave Lucy a dirty look.

"Bless you," he said sarcastically. He had his hands on his hips.

"Sorry," said Lucy. She slunk back to her side of the banquette.

"Good going," Joey whispered to her. "That was cool."

"I didn't mean to do it. It was an accident."

"My kind of accident," said Joey. He gave Lucy a hug.

Albert and Spider finished their game. Their score was twenty points higher than Lucy and Joey's. But Lucy and Joey still had a frame to go.

Joey was working on a spare in his final frame. "Go, Joey, go," shouted Lucy happily.

"Don't get me nervous," snapped Joey. "Let me concentrate."

Joey squinted down the alley. He let go of the ball a moment too soon. It dribbled into the gutter.

"Come on, Lucy. You can still win it for us," said Joey, handing her the ball. "If you get a strike, we can beat them by three points. We'll win the prize. Don't let me down."

"Pressure, pressure!" taunted Albert from the sidelines.

Lucy felt as if the whole party were looking at her. She thought about how much Joey wanted to win. He had even told his father about it.

Suddenly the lights in the bowling alley flickered.

"Hey," shouted Melanie, "it must be time for the cake."

Lucy let the ball go. It went straight down the middle.

The lights flickered again. Lucy glanced over her shoulder. Everyone at the party had their backs to her as they looked toward the rear to see whether the cake was really coming out or not.

Lucy watched her ball. It caught seven pins, leaving three pins standing.

Then the sweeper came down.

"Hey, Lucy," said Melanie. "What did you get? I didn't see, and the electronic scorer went on the blink."

Lucy hesitated. Her throat felt dry. Her stomach cramped.

"I got a strike," lied Lucy.

"I knew you could do it," shouted Melanie.

Melanie's mother came over with two large boxes.

"For the winners," she said. She was laughing.

Albert gave Joey a kind of funny look. "Hey, man, you won. I guess winning's everything."

"Aren't you happy?" Lucy whispered to Joey. "We won."

Melanie handed them each an identical white box with a silver ribbon around it.

Lucy opened her box first. She pulled out a black-and-white bowling shirt with the word "Boogie's" written in script in glitter. It showed a diner with the motto "Eat Heavy, Dress Cool" in a bubble. The motto was written out in silver studs.

Joey opened his box. It was an identical shirt.

Lucy hesitated a moment. She saw Melanie looking at them. Melanie had made such a big deal out of the prize, and it was a shirt. A cool-looking shirt, but just a shirt.

Joey grinned at Melanie. "Absolutely great," he said.

Melanie breathed a sigh of relief, and Lucy realized she had been holding her breath, too.

Everybody walked over to the cafeteria where Melanie had set up place cards.

Joey went off somewhere. Lucy saw him talking with Albert. Joey was the last person to sit down.

"What did you do with your present?" Lucy asked. She had slipped on the bowling shirt over her shirt.

"I took it off," said Joey. He took a piece of pizza and stuffed it in his mouth.

Lucy had no appetite for the pizza.

Finally, it was time for Melanie to open her presents.

When she opened the box from Lucy, she held the crystal up to the light.

"Lucy, Joey, it's so beautiful," said Melanie.

"It's supposed to have magical powers," said Lucy. "I mean, it'll bring you luck."

"Hey," shouted Albert, "if that thing will help me pass Mr. Vega's tests, then I want a piece of it."

"No way," said Melanie, putting the crystal around her neck. "That would be cheating."

Lucy felt her cheeks flame red.

"Nice present," said Joey.

She took a deep breath. She had gotten away with it. It was stupid to worry. Cheating on her bowling score had made Joey happy. They had won. It was worth it.

15

After the opening of the presents, the party wound down. Lucy felt as deflated as one of Melanie's birthday balloons. She had a headache. She couldn't believe that she had cheated at her best friend's birthday party. Not only had she cheated, but now she didn't feel too well, either.

She sat on the bench and took off her bowling shoes. Albert came by. "My mom's here," he said. "She's giving us a ride home."

"Where's Joey?" Lucy asked.

"He's already in the car," said Albert. "We'll meet you outside."

Lucy took her shoes and put them on the counter and got her own shoes back. Her "date" hadn't even bothered to tell her he was leaving.

She walked into the parking lot. Spider waved

to her from the back seat of a small beige Honda. Spider got out, and Lucy was wedged into the middle of the back seat between Joey and Spider.

Albert was in the front with his mother, a surprisingly small woman with a warm smile. "I'm so glad Albert's meeting such nice friends at his new school," she said. "You know, he was very nervous about going to junior high."

Lucy glanced at Albert. It was hard to imagine him nervous about anything — even failing Mr. Vega's class.

"Put on your seat belt, Albert," said Mrs. Barber. Albert did it dutifully.

"Hey, Ma," said Albert, "drive carefully. In the back seat, you are carrying the grand champions of the bowling party — Lucy and Joey. Don't those names sound good together?"

"I love the name Lucy," said Mrs. Barber. "When I was a kid, I used to watch *I Love Lucy* reruns. She just cracked me up."

"Well, Lucy is Joey's favorite comedienne, isn't she?" said Albert. His voice had a needling quality to it.

Joey sat with his arms crossed staring out the window.

"Shut up, Albert," he said.

"What's the matter? Aren't you glad we won?" Lucy asked Joey.

Joey grunted something. Lucy thought it was a yes.

"I think the shirts are adorable," said Spider. "I really wish that we had won. We came so close, Albert."

"Yeah, well, in a fair fight we would have," said Albert.

Lucy felt her cheeks flame. "What does that mean, Albert?" she demanded.

"He's just trying to bait you," whispered Spider. "He hates to lose. Don't pay him any attention."

"Albert," warned Mrs. Barber, "be nice."

"I'm always nice," said Albert. Lucy sat on the hump with her knees practically hitting her chin. Had Albert guessed she had cheated?

Lucy took a deep breath. Her father had always told her to count to ten before she lost her temper.

Lucy got to six, but she was still angry. Half of her realized it wasn't Albert's fault. He was making all these innuendos, and Joey was just sitting there like stone.

Did Joey know that she had cheated? She told herself she was overreacting. Nothing that Albert said implied that he really knew anything. Albert just liked to tease. It was in his nature.

Lucy snuck glances at Joey, hoping for a clue about his feelings, but he just stared out the window as if he had never seen a mall or a McDonald's restaurant in his life.

Finally Joey spoke up. "You should drop Lucy off first," he said to Albert's mother. "Her house is the most convenient."

Logically, it would have made much more sense to drop Spider off, and then Joey, but it was as if Joey couldn't stand the idea of being in the car with her one more moment than necessary.

Lucy wished that Joey would stick up for her — tell Albert to stick it in his ear. Why couldn't he say, "Hey Albert, lay off"? But Joey didn't say more than six words the entire ride home.

When they got to Lucy's house, Joey got out of the car and walked her to the door.

"Well, we're winners," said Lucy, knowing that her voice sounded phony. "You can tell your father that we won. He'll like that."

"Yeah," said Joey, "he'll like it."

"What's the matter, Joey?" Lucy couldn't help asking. She had to know if he knew that she had cheated. Was that why he was mad at her?

"Nothing," said Joey. "Why do you think something's wrong?"

"No reason," said Lucy, feeling like a coward. Now she was a coward and a cheater.

16

On Monday when Lucy got to school, Melanie was wearing the crystal around her neck. "I really loved your present," she said. Lucy put her jacket in her locker. She looked around the hall. She didn't see Joey.

"How come you're not wearing your winning bowling shirt to school?" asked Melanie. "Didn't you like the prize? Was it special enough? You seemed so quiet after you won."

"It was beautiful," said Lucy.

"Are you okay, Lucy? You're acting strange."

"I'm fine," said Lucy.

Joey walked to his locker. He opened it without looking at them once.

"Did you and Joey have a fight?" Melanie asked.

Lucy shrugged. "No."

"He's not wearing the shirt, either," said Melanie. "I was sure you two would wear the matching shirts to school." Melanie sounded hurt.

"We both liked the shirts, okay?" snapped Lucy.

"Something weird is happening, isn't it?" said Melanie. "Is it about my party? Did people not have a good time? Tell me the truth."

"It was a great party, Melanie. Honest."

"You mean it?" asked Melanie.

"Yes," Lucy nodded. She couldn't believe that things had gotten so complicated that she had to reassure Melanie about her party — Melanie, who had never met a birthday party that she didn't like — especially her own.

Joey walked by them with his head down. "Hi, Joey," said Melanie. "Congratulations!"

Joey looked up. "On what?" he asked.

"Winning at my party, dodo!" teased Melanie.

Joey practically ran down the hall.

"Now what's with him?" Melanie insisted.

"I don't know," said Lucy. "Don't ask me to understand boys. You were the one who got us into this."

"Me? What did I do?"

"You made it a couples-only party," screeched Lucy. "That was the stupidest idea you've ever had." Lucy slammed her locker shut.

The bell rang for classes. All day Lucy felt as

if she were traveling in a black cloud. Melanie was barely talking to her. Joey wasn't talking to her at all.

Finally, the day was over and it was time for basketball practice. Lucy wondered what she could do to foul up basketball practice, too.

Mr. Vega started them with one-on-one drills, pitting Spider and Lucy against each other. They both played aggressively. Spider rushed forward, placing herself squarely in front of Lucy.

Lucy stole the ball from her. She moved her head to the left. Spider fell for the fake. Lucy triumphantly dribbled the ball right by her.

Mr. Vega blew his whistle. "Good fake, Lucy. Excellent. You're turning into a very sneaky player. I like it. Take a rest."

Lucy flopped down on the sidelines, but she felt good. Her mind felt sharp, as if the black cloud had lifted.

Spider plopped down next to her. "Watch it. You're getting a little too sneaky."

Lucy punched Spider on the arm playfully.

"I'm not kidding," said Spider. "First, you cheated to win the bowling prize . . ."

Lucy felt as if the blood had stopped moving in her body. It was the feeling that she had had as a little kid when she fell off a swing and had all the air knocked out of her.

Lucy looked so angry that Spider flinched.

"Hey, *I* didn't call you a cheater — Joey and Albert did," said Spider. "I thought you knew."

"*Joey*'s calling me a cheater?" Lucy managed to gasp.

"Actually," said Spider, matter-of-factly, "it was Albert who saw you cheat. Albert was being kind of nice. He thought it would be mean to make a big deal out of it in front of Melanie. It was her party. You know, Albert really does have a soft heart. He doesn't look it, but . . ."

Spider stopped. Lucy was standing up, holding her stomach.

"What's wrong?"

"I'm sick," said Lucy. "Tell Coach Vega for me, please. Tell him I got a stomachache."

Lucy ran into the locker room. She locked herself into a bathroom and clutched her stomach.

Finally, she pulled herself together. She changed into her street clothes and pushed out of the locker room. She almost flung the door in the face of Mr. Vega.

"Lucy, are you feeling all right?" he asked. "Spider told me you were sick."

"I got a stomachache," said Lucy quickly. Mr. Vega was the last person she wanted to talk to.

"It came on awfully suddenly," said Mr. Vega.

Lucy wondered if he knew she was lying. Great. Now she was a cheater and a liar — all because of Joey.

"Are your eyes okay?" asked Mr. Vega.

Lucy rubbed them. "It's just an allergy attack," she said quickly, anything to get away from there.

"Well, I just wanted to check that you were all right. You played well today. I was proud of you."

Lucy was worried that she was going to yell "how can you be proud of a cheater?" at Mr. Vega. Instead she bit the inside of her lip.

Mr. Vega turned and went back out to the basketball court.

Lucy roamed the halls, looking for Joey. Finally, she found him alone by his locker.

Joey kept his head down.

"Joey," shouted Lucy.

"What?" he asked. He sounded annoyed that she was bothering him.

Lucy felt deflated. "Joey, what's going on?"

"Nothing," mumbled Joey.

"That's not true," said Lucy. "Spider just told me that you think I cheated on my bowling score just so that we could win."

"It's embarrassing," said Joey.

"But if you thought I cheated, why didn't you

say something to me!" Lucy's voice ended in a high-pitched squeak.

"I didn't want to embarrass you," said Joey.

"Embarrass me?" said Lucy. She knew she was shrieking, but she couldn't help herself. "What could be more embarrassing than hearing on the basketball court that you think I'm a cheater?"

"Keep your voice down, will you?" said Joey. He sounded really angry. "You're making a scene."

"Spider said you said I was too sneaky. That's awful." Lucy was near tears.

"Shhh," said Joey. His voice sounded as if he were pleading with her. "Albert saw you cheat when we won. He kept quiet about it because he didn't want to upset Melanie, but he told me he definitely saw you cheat."

"Yeah, yeah," said Lucy. "I know all about what a nice guy Albert is."

Joey shrugged. "Well, I think it was kind of decent of him. But he told me that he knew, and it really made me feel creepy."

"How do you think it makes me feel having everybody know I'm a cheater?" hissed Lucy.

"You did cheat, didn't you?" asked Joey. "You never said that Albert was lying."

Lucy blinked. She could have denied the

whole thing, but now it was too late. Joey wouldn't believe her. Why should he? The truth was that she had cheated. She shook her head. "I don't believe this is happening to me."

"Believe it," said Joey. "You're the one who's the cheater."

Lucy stared at the ground, fighting back the urge to cry. She had imagined somehow that confronting Joey would make everything all right, but it wasn't.

There was nothing she could do to erase the words, "You did cheat."

17

Lucy spent the night in her room, pretending to do her homework, but basically she just stared at her books, imagining Joey telling everybody he met that he was embarrassed to go out with a girl who cheated.

Every time Lucy thought about people at school knowing that she cheated, she wanted to cry. Finally, she put her books away. Studying was hopeless. She got in bed and did something that she used to do as a kid. She put the covers up over her head.

In the morning, she decided she just couldn't face it. "I'm too sick to go to school," she announced at breakfast. "I'm going back to bed, okay?"

Her father felt her forehead. "You feel cool," he said.

Lucy looked at her father indignantly.

"She did look terrible yesterday, Len," said Lucy's mother. "You didn't see her when she came home from basketball practice. She was clammy."

"Get back in bed. Let me take your temperature," said her father. Lucy took the thermometer and put it in her mouth. She pressed down with her tongue, hoping the pressure would help bring her temperature up.

Her father picked up her science book. "Chaos," he said. "I've read about this."

Lucy made a strange humming sound. She wondered why people tried to talk to you when you couldn't.

Her father looked at his watch. "Just sixty more seconds. I'll go get my coffee."

As soon as her father left the room, Lucy took the thermometer out of her mouth. The number flashing was 95.2, but 98.6 was normal. She was way below normal.

Quickly Lucy took the thermometer and rubbed it on her blanket. The friction brought the thermometer up to 101.2. Lucy wondered if this could qualify as a science experiment.

She stuck it back in her mouth just as her father came back into the room, carrying a coffee cup.

He took the thermometer out and checked it.

He looked into Lucy's eyes. "You *do* have a temperature," he said. He felt her forehead again.

"I told you," said Lucy sullenly.

She slipped back under the covers, pulling them up. "Can I have the TV in my room?"

"I think you should just rest. You'll probably sleep."

Lucy shook her head. She knew she wouldn't sleep. She wanted something to shut up the anxiety in her head, the chatter in her brain.

After her father went to work, her mother came in to see her with a little tea and toast.

"I thought maybe this would settle your stomach," she said.

Lucy was starving. She nibbled on the toast, trying not to show how hungry she was.

"Thanks, Mom. I'm feeling a little better."

"Lucy, are you sure you're okay? I mean, really. You seem depressed."

"I read somewhere that being sick *does* make you depressed," argued Lucy.

"It was probably in one of my articles," said her mom. Lucy often forgot that her mother *did* have a sense of humor.

Her mother sighed and smoothed a piece of hair from Lucy's face. "Well, you rest today. I have to deliver my column to the paper this morning and then I have a meeting. Will you be all right in the house alone? Do you want me to cancel my appointments?"

"No," said Lucy quickly. "I'll be fine."

"Lucy, you know you can tell me anything. There's nothing you would ever do that would make me not love you."

"Mom, what are you thinking?" asked Lucy.

"Nothing," said her mom. "I just know something's bothering you."

"I am just sick," protested Lucy.

Her mom nodded. As she started to leave the room, Lucy stopped her. "Mom, did you ever do something so embarrassing that you wanted to die?"

Her mother sat down on the edge of the bed. "Well, when I was about your age, I was a little flat-chested."

"Tell me about it," said Lucy. "I inherited it."

"I know," said her mom, "only now it's a little more fashionable. Back when I was a teenager, everyone wanted big boobs. Anyhow, my mother wouldn't buy me a padded bra. She didn't believe in them. So I stuffed my bra with socks, and while I was dancing with this boy I had a crush on, his name was Stevie Biltekoff, Stevie saw a sock in the middle of my breasts. One of the socks had slipped. He took it out and waved it to his friend."

"What a jerk," said Lucy.

"Now, it's easy to say that. Back then, I just wanted to die."

"Did you ever tell him what you thought about him?"

Her mother laughed. "Yeah, at my twentieth high school reunion last year."

"Did he remember doing it to you?" Lucy asked.

"Not only did he remember, but he felt bad about it for twenty years. I ended up comforting him and it wasn't that big a deal. Plus he had gotten a real potbelly. He made your dad look good."

Her mother looked at her watch.

"I'd better go. Are you sure you'll be all right alone?"

"I'm sure, Mom," said Lucy.

The house seemed so quiet. Lucy wondered if this was how real nightmares happened. You did something in a split second that you had to live with the rest of your life.

She picked up her science book and started to study chaos.

Finally around three-thirty, the doorbell rang.

Melanie was at the door.

She looked serious, for Melanie. Lucy let her in.

"I brought you your homework," said Melanie.

"Did I miss a quiz from Mr. Vega?" Lucy asked, leafing through the pages.

Melanie shook her head.

"Maybe I'll be sick tomorrow, too," said Lucy.

"You can't stay sick forever," said Melanie.

"I might," said Lucy. Lucy paused. She had always been able to talk to Melanie about everything, but this seemed so humiliating.

"So . . ." Lucy stopped. She couldn't just chatter. Melanie was her best friend. "Mel, I don't know what to do," Lucy began softly.

"About being sick?" asked Melanie.

"No, about . . ." Lucy paused, " . . . about Joey. Spider told me that everyone knows."

"Spider loves to gossip," said Melanie.

"Do you know Joey says that I cheated at your party?" Lucy asked.

Melanie nodded.

"I did cheat," confessed Lucy.

"Why?" asked Melanie.

Lucy closed her eyes. "I thought it would make Joey like me more. His father cares so much about winning. I thought he wanted to bring back a prize. So now he's telling everybody I'm a cheater. You probably won't want a cheater as a friend."

"Cheating on bowling isn't exactly on my list

of the seven deadly sins," said Melanie.

"Are you mad at me?"

"Well, I wanted you to win the shirt. I'm not sure I wanted you to cheat, lie, and steal to get it."

"I didn't lie or steal. I just cheated."

"It was a figure of speech. I think you're taking this a little too seriously."

"This from you. You hate cheaters. In fourth grade, you turned in Allison Ellman for cheating on a test."

"Yeah, and everyone hated me for it . . . said I was a tattletale."

"Don't you want to give me a lecture about cheating?" asked Lucy.

"I wouldn't know what to say," said Melanie, sounding embarrassed. "It's so stupid."

Lucy started to laugh. "Yeah, I'm going to go through life branded as a cheater because of bowling. I don't even like to bowl."

"I don't think that's the issue," said Melanie quietly. "You've got to go to school tomorrow. You can't hide in your house forever."

18

It was Wednesday morning, and Lucy couldn't believe that just over a week ago, the worst thing she had to face was one of Mr. Vega's pop quizzes. Lucy knew that Melanie was right. She couldn't hide and pretend she was sick forever. She knew she'd have to go back to school.

"Just my luck," thought Lucy as she got dressed. "I'll get up my nerve to go to school and Mr. Vega will give me a pop quiz."

At breakfast she told her parents that she felt well enough to go to school.

"Are you sure you're all right?" Lucy's father asked. Lucy tried to read if there was anything sarcastic in his voice, but she didn't think so.

"I'm fine," she said.

Her mother felt her forehead. "You're as cool as a cucumber," she said.

"Or a pickle," said Lucy. "A pickle is a cucumber — why don't people say cool as a pickle?"

"Are you in some kind of pickle?" teased her dad.

"Not exactly," said Lucy.

Her mother glanced up. "You know, you've hardly mentioned Melanie's party. I know you and Joey won the grand prize, but . . ."

"Please don't mention Joey's name to me," snapped Lucy.

Lucy's mother and father exchanged looks. "And don't give me a lecture about what a nice boy he is," added Lucy.

Lucy slammed her plate into the sink and started to stalk out of the kitchen. "Lucy!" shouted her father.

Lucy took a deep breath. "Sorry," she said. "I'm still getting over the twenty-four-hour flu or whatever it was I had."

"*That's* no excuse," said her father.

Her mother was studying her. "What?" Lucy demanded.

"Nothing," said her mother. "You'd better get going — the school bus will be here soon."

"Mom, if you dare say anything about teenage problems, I'll strangle you."

"That's no way to talk to your mother," warned her father.

"It's all right, Len," said Lucy's mother. "Honest, it is all right."

Lucy swallowed. "Mom, I'm sorry I said that. I didn't mean I'd strangle you."

"I know. Being a teenager *is* hard. It's a lot to sort out. After all, I've written columns about it." Her mother grinned to show she was teasing.

Lucy laughed. She couldn't believe she could still laugh.

When she got on the bus, Spider was sitting with Albert.

"Hey, Lucy!" shouted Albert. "Feeling better?"

"Yeah," said Lucy, taking a seat.

"I bet," said Albert, winking at her.

Spider poked him with her elbow.

Melanie got on the bus and sat next to Lucy. "Thanks," said Lucy.

"For what?" asked Melanie.

"For sitting next to a cheater," said Lucy.

Melanie rolled her eyes. "This is getting boring," she said. "It was *my* birthday party, and it's been upstaged by your little melodrama."

"You're right as usual," said Lucy.

"It's boring being right," said Melanie.

In school, Lucy didn't even catch sight of Joey until just before Mr. Vega's class. He tried to walk past her. As Mr. Vega came by, Lucy didn't realize that she was standing in front of the doorway to the room. "Excuse me," said Mr. Vega, trying to get into his own classroom.

Lucy jumped out of the way. "I'm glad you're feeling better," said Mr. Vega, but he gave Lucy a funny look.

"I wonder if he's heard that I'm a cheater, too," mumbled Lucy bitterly.

"Not from me," said Joey. "I didn't tell him."

Lucy opened her mouth and shut it. "Why did you have to tell *anybody*?" she asked. Her words came out in one long whine.

Joey just gave her a disgusted look and walked into class.

Dustin bumped into Lucy as she took her seat.

"Are you okay?" Dustin asked.

"Why shouldn't I be?" Lucy asked.

"You were sick yesterday," said Dustin. He put his books down on his desk. "You look sick now."

Lucy just shook her head. Mr. Vega called for attention.

"Good morning, girls and boys. Today you're going to have a pop quiz."

"I don't see why you don't give us a warning," groused Lucy. "It's not fair."

"Then it wouldn't be a pop quiz," said Mr. Vega. "We've been studying patterns — the unseen patterns in what look like random events."

"You mean there is an order to this torture?" said Joey.

"Very good, Mr. Rich," said Mr. Vega. "You're actually thinking today. Good, I like that in a student."

Mr. Vega handed out the test questions. Lucy looked down at the test. She felt as if everybody was staring at her — as if she were wearing a big C for cheater on her back.

She looked down at her test:

The Butterfly Effect is

A) *David Ruelle's idea for turbulence.*
B) *a scientific discovery used by Olympic swimmers.*
C) *Lorenz's rule for order masquerading as randomness.*
D) *the effect that a butterfly's wings have on the weather.*

Dustin was working on his paper, angling it toward her again. Lucy saw that he had circled D. She bit her lip. She would have picked A as her choice. She was already branded a cheater — why shouldn't she just glance at Dustin's paper? Mr. Vega had his back to the class, writing something on the chalkboard.

Even Mr. Vega didn't have eyes in the back of his head.

Lucy sighed.

She shook her head. She ignored Dustin's paper and circled A, her original answer.

She didn't care if she flunked. She didn't care about anything, but just because she had been labeled a cheater didn't mean that she had to cheat by copying from Dustin.

She wouldn't cheat.

19

Mr. Vega waited until Friday to hand back the quizzes.

"These tests were very disappointing," he said. He paused. "Again. Apparently you students think that science is a bunch of facts to memorize — no, no . . . I need you thinking. I need alert minds."

He handed back the papers. "Lucy, you aren't even trying to apply your brain," he said.

Lucy turned the paper over. An F.

"Good work, Dustin," said Mr. Vega. He finished passing out the corrected tests.

"All right," said Mr. Vega. "I'll go over the correct answers. Number one, the Butterfly Effect."

Dustin raised his hand. "D," he answered. "If a butterfly beats its wings in China — it could change the weather here in Indianapolis. It was the beginning of chaos theory."

"That's why we have the worst weather in the world," said Albert. "Too many butterflies in China."

"Albert, when you pull your grade up to passing level, you can make all the jokes you want. I'll give you the floor for a comic hour — but as for now, shut up and learn," said Mr. Vega.

At the end of class, Lucy had marked all the right answers on her quiz.

She walked out of class with her head down. Joey and Albert were talking in front of her.

"I got an F minus," said Albert. "Whoever heard of an F minus?"

Joey crumpled his paper. "I flunked again, too. My dad will kill me."

"F minus," said Melanie to Albert. "I didn't know there was a grade below F."

"What did you get, Melanie?" asked Joey.

"B plus," said Melanie. "How did you do, Lucy?"

"I flunked," said Lucy. "At least it's proof I didn't cheat."

"I got a B," said Dustin. He gave Lucy a funny look. "Lucy, you should have done better. You're usually smarter than that."

"Smarter or sneakier," said Albert.

"Albert Barber, shut up," said Dustin. "Lucy was a terrific girl in our old school."

Lucy didn't know whether to cry or laugh. It was nice to be reminded that at least she hadn't always been labeled a cheater and a liar.

"Thanks, Dustin," said Lucy. "It's okay."

"It's not okay," said Spider. "If you don't get your grades up, you're gonna be off the basketball team. You can't play sports unless you get a C average in all your courses."

"What did you get?" Lucy asked her.

"C minus. I'm into sneaking by."

They walked down the hall. "Thanks for sticking up for me," Lucy said to Dustin.

"Ever since you started going out with that Joey guy, it's like you're just not there. But I remember the old Lucy."

Lucy sighed. "I don't go with him. You must be the one person in the world who doesn't know he broke up with me because I cheated at bowling."

"I did hear about it," muttered Dustin.

"Thanks for not mentioning it. I didn't cheat on the exam. I didn't look at your test."

"I know that," said Dustin. "After all, you flunked, and I got a B. Do you want to study together?"

"Would you really help me?" Lucy asked.

"Yeah," said Dustin. "I think I learn better when I study with someone else. And who else *is* there? Melanie's way smarter than me. I can't keep up with her."

It wasn't very flattering, but at least studying with Dustin might pull up her grade.

Up ahead, Melanie was walking with Joey and Albert. Lucy was so shocked to see them together that she didn't know what to do. Melanie was throwing her head back and laughing at something that Albert said.

Lucy was sure it was a joke about her.

She pretended to be fumbling with her locker.

Melanie broke off from the two boys and came over to Lucy. "You know Joey and Albert really do have a good sense of humor."

"How can you talk to them, Melanie? Joey's the one who is calling me a cheater."

Melanie opened her locker. "You did cheat. You told me so."

"Yeah, but you were the one who said it wasn't a big deal."

"It isn't," said Melanie. "But it doesn't mean that I can't talk to Joey. He's a nice guy."

"Nice!" Lucy practically squawked. "He's telling everyone I'm a cheater."

Melanie just gave Lucy a long look.

Lucy sighed again. "All right, yes, I am a cheater — what does everyone want me to do, wear a big C all the time?"

"Just stop talking about it so much," said Melanie. "Joey asked if I'd help him and Albert study. They want to pull up their grade in Mr. Vega's class. I said I had to ask you first. Do you mind?"

Lucy did mind. "Melanie, they're creeps," she blurted out. "You were the one who came over yesterday and said you were my friend. That meant so much to me."

"I am your friend," protested Melanie. "I'm just going to help Joey and Albert study."

"I'll give you a hint," said Lucy bitterly.

"What's the hint?" asked Melanie.

"Don't cheat," said Lucy.

Melanie stared at her. "Why would I do that?"

"That's what I'm asking *myself*," said Lucy.

20

On Saturday, Dustin was true to his word and came over to study with Lucy.

"Hi, Dustin," said Lucy's mother. "I haven't seen you in a while."

"He's just here to study, Mom," said Lucy, not wanting her mother to get any cute ideas. "We've got to do some experiments."

Dustin looked down at his sheet. "We need to go outside. I came over here because you have a swing still up in your yard."

Mrs. Lovello smiled. "That swing has such sentimental value to me."

"Face it, Mom, you just like to go swing on it sometimes. And so do I," admitted Lucy.

Lucy's mother nodded.

Lucy and Dustin went outside. Most of the leaves on the trees had blown away. There was a chill in the air. Lucy shivered.

"We're supposed to be studying the gravitational pull of weight as it affects the pendulum," said Dustin.

"It already sounds too hard for me," said Lucy.

Dustin took hold of the swing. "Count how many times it swings back and forth when I let it go."

"This is homework?" asked Lucy. Her head swiveled back and forth as she counted the swings. "Thirteen!" she cried out.

"Now we have to count it when there is weight on the swing. Get on," said Dustin. Lucy sat down on the swing.

"I've got a digital watch. I'll set the stopwatch," said Dustin as he pulled the swing back to his waist and then let it go. Lucy swung back and forth. She felt as if her chest had turned to stone. She couldn't imagine laughing like a kid again, giggling and not worrying that everybody thought you were a cheater.

"Did you count?" Dustin asked.

Lucy shook her head. She had been too engrossed in feeling sorry for herself.

"We'll have to do it over again," complained Dustin.

Lucy got back on the swing. She felt Dustin pull her back. For ten seconds, she counted the swings. Then gradually the swing came to a dead stop.

"That was thirteen!" she exclaimed. "It wasn't any less than when there was nobody on the swing. That's amazing."

"But the speed changed," added Dustin. "You didn't go as fast as the swing without any weight."

"It's not what I would have expected," said Lucy, looking back at the swing.

"It's not supposed to be," said Dustin. "That's what I like about science. It's not always what you expect."

"Nothing's ever what it seems," said Lucy with a sigh.

"We're not here to philosophize," said Dustin, writing down the results of their experiment. "We're here to study."

"Okay, what's next?" asked Lucy.

Dustin looked annoyed. "Don't you check the homework assignments at all?" he said. "We're studying molecular wave action and turbulence."

Lucy sank down on the grass.

"Turbulence, I know," she said with a sigh. "It was the Butterfly Effect that got me down."

"The Butterfly Effect is the theory that small

errors can be catastrophic," said Dustin. "It's my favorite."

"Right, like changing one stupid bowling score — that's going to haunt me the rest of my life."

Dustin looked bored. "I didn't come over here to talk about your bowling score — or Joey Rich. I came to study. If you don't want to do that, I'll go home."

Lucy shook her head. "I don't want you to do that," she admitted. The experiments were starting to be a little bit interesting. It was also more fun being with Dustin than with Joey. She didn't feel as if he were judging her all the time.

But Lucy couldn't stop thinking about Joey. It bothered her that he might be studying with Melanie right at this moment and the two of them could be talking about her.

"*Lucy,*" said Dustin, starting to sound annoyed. "We need a tennis ball for the next experiment. We have to put it in the freezer."

Lucy took a phosphorescent-yellow ball and stuck it in the freezer. She took out a half-gallon of chocolate crunch and one of boysenberry sherbet.

"I've got another experiment for while we're waiting," said Lucy. "Which will go faster? The chocolate crunch or the boysenberry?"

"Why not have both?" said Dustin. "It can be a study of strange attractors. That's another one of our chapters."

Lucy got out her book. As she read over the chapter with Dustin, it began to make sense.

Lucy took careful notes.

Before she knew it, the alarm on Dustin's watch went off.

Lucy went to the freezer. She took out the tennis ball, which felt brittle — as if it would break.

"It feels strange," said Lucy.

"Cold does weird things to all matter," said Dustin. "That's in this book, too."

Lucy held a yardstick up, and Dustin let the ball drop.

It landed with a thud and bounced back only about twelve inches.

"It's only got about a third of the bounce it did before," said Lucy.

"Yes, but why?" asked Dustin.

Lucy squinted her eyes and tried to remember what she and Dustin had just studied in the book.

"Because the chains of molecules become rigid when the ball is chilled," repeated Lucy.

"Good," said Dustin. "Now give a practical application. Mr. Vega loves those."

"If you play baseball on a really cold day, you have to take into account that the ball won't go as far."

"Right," said Dustin. "It's why home-run hitters love to play on hot nights. The ball carries farther."

"So what does this have to do with chaos?" asked Lucy.

"Because everything is always in the process of changing," said Dustin. "As we speak, the ball is warming up. Try it again."

Lucy let the ball go. Now it bounced back up to nearly twenty-six inches.

"See? It rebounds. Scientists used to think that everything could be measured exactly, and they'd always be able to predict the future — but it's not true."

"I'm glad," said Lucy.

"What do you mean?" asked Dustin.

"If you could predict my future from my first month at junior high, my life would be a disaster."

"Or if you could predict when Mr. Vega was going to give an exam."

"There are patterns," said Lucy. "I mean, the

ball does bounce higher as it gets warmer."

"Patterns," repeated Dustin.

"Do you remember what Mr. Vega said to you before the last exam? Something about a pattern in chaos?" said Lucy.

"We had the first pop quiz on a Monday — this last one was on a Wednesday. Maybe he gives one to us every week, but the day that it will be on changes — Monday, Wednesday, and then he'd skip a day. We'd get another one next week on a Friday."

Dustin shook his head. "That's too simple."

"Simple, but elegant. Isn't that what great science is supposed to be?" asked Lucy.

"You know," said Dustin. "That could be just the way Mr. Vega's fiendish mind would work. He would pick something really easy, like skipping a day every week, and not tell us about it."

"If I'm right, at least we'd know when the next quiz is coming."

"It's still guesswork," said Dustin.

"It's a probability," said Lucy, opening her book. "After all, I can't do worse than an F."

"Yes, you can," said Dustin. "Remember, Albert got an F minus."

21

After Dustin left, Lucy picked up the phone to call Melanie, but then she thought about Melanie studying with Joey. She put down the receiver. Only after the weekend was over did Lucy realize that Melanie hadn't called her, either. It was the first weekend since they were really little that they hadn't talked to each other on the phone.

On Monday at school, Lucy was about to say something to Melanie when Joey came up to ask Melanie a question about Mr. Vega's homework.

Lucy felt herself blush and quickly moved away. Melanie watched her. When Joey walked down the hall, Melanie came over to her.

"Why did you walk away?" she asked.

"I didn't, exactly," stammered Lucy. "I just wanted to look at the bulletin board."

Melanie looked up at the bulletin board,

which gave directions for a fire drill.

"Yeah, right," said Melanie.

"Well, you never know when there's going to be a fire drill," said Lucy defensively. "So what's it like tutoring Joey Rich?"

"I don't exactly tutor him. I just help him out a little. How was it studying with Dustin? Do you like him? Maybe the two of you could be a couple. I wouldn't mind. Dustin and I aren't really right for each other."

"Oh, and you and Joey are?" asked Lucy sarcastically.

"That's not what I meant."

"Melanie, you've gone boy crazy."

"I just asked you if you liked Dustin," protested Melanie.

"I like basketball. I'd like to pass Mr. Vega's science class. Those are my two likes."

"You've got no right to call me boy crazy," said Melanie indignantly. "I didn't *cheat* to impress a boy."

"Give it a rest, Melanie," said Lucy as she walked away from Melanie and toward her next class.

Melanie didn't call Lucy that night or the next night, either.

Lucy used the time to study.

She even took her books down to the locker room during basketball practice.

"It's good to have you back," said Mr. Vega to Lucy. "You're feeling better?"

"Yes," said Lucy.

"Today, we're going to practice no-look passes," said Mr. Vega. "I want you to split into four lines. If your first name has an even number of letters in it, you'll pass to the left. Odd numbers pass to the right."

"Nicknames or real names?" asked Spider.

"It's your choice," said Mr. Vega. "The point is, I don't want the person catching your pass to know when it's coming. You have to learn to sense when a pass is coming. Let's make this quick! Quick!"

Lucy lined up, but her mind wasn't working well. She forgot that she had an even number in her name and passed to the wrong row.

"Lucy! Four letters! It's not hard!"

"Sorry," said Lucy.

Mr. Vega shook his head. "Just concentrate, please!"

The practice seemed to last forever. Finally, it was over and they filed into the locker room.

Spider stood by Lucy's bench. She picked up Lucy's science book.

"Are you trying to impress Mr. Vega?" she asked.

"No," said Lucy. "I'm just trying to pass science."

"Try passing me the ball some more. You acted like a zombie out there on the court."

Lucy sighed and closed the book. Spider was right. She hadn't been very good in practice.

"Do you think Mr. Vega noticed?" she asked Spider.

"I think he notices everything," said Spider.

22

For the rest of the week, there were no pop quizzes from Mr. Vega. Then on Monday, once again, no pop quiz. On Tuesday, no pop quiz; none on Wednesday or Thursday, either.

"I told you," Lucy said to Dustin. "It's going to be Friday. I'm sure of it."

"I'm not," said Dustin, but he agreed to study more than usual. Lucy spent all of Thursday evening going over her science book. Melanie still didn't call. A couple of times, Lucy picked up the phone to call Melanie, but then she decided against it.

On Friday before Mr. Vega's class, Melanie passed Lucy in the hall. "Hi," she said.

"Hi," said Lucy, hugging her books and looking down.

"Look . . . " Melanie said nervously. She didn't get a chance to finish her sentence.

Dustin came up to Lucy. "You ready, Lucy?" he asked.

"Ready for what?" asked Melanie.

"We think Mr. Vega's going to pull a pop quiz today." Dustin turned to Melanie. "We figured out a pattern."

Melanie stared at them. "Are you sure?"

Her question annoyed Lucy. "Do you think you have the only brain around here? I have one, too."

"I know that," said Melanie. "But do you think there's going to be a test today?"

"I'm not one hundred percent sure, but it's a big probability," said Lucy proudly. She was about to launch into an explanation for her theory when Joey and Albert came up.

"What's a probability?" asked Albert. Joey didn't even say hello to Lucy.

"Lucy and Dustin say that they know Mr. Vega's gonna pull a pop quiz today," said Melanie. Lucy gave Melanie a dirty look.

Joey and Albert looked at each other. "Melanie, we've got to see you. Quick."

"Not now," hissed Melanie.

"We can't take the chance," whispered Albert. He grabbed Melanie by the upper arm and moved her a few feet down the hall. Lucy followed them with her eyes.

"Come on," said Dustin. "You don't have to worry about them."

"What do you think they wanted Melanie for?" Lucy asked.

"It's not your problem," insisted Dustin. He steered Lucy into the classroom.

Lucy took her seat. After a minute, Joey took his seat next to Lucy. He was fidgeting, playing with his shoes, looking around the room. He seemed to want to look anywhere but at Lucy.

Mr. Vega opened the door. "Good morning," he said. "Everybody settle down. Today we'll have a pop quiz."

Lucy's mouth dropped open. She had been right. Dustin grinned at her. Lucy smiled back. She was proud of herself.

As Mr. Vega handed her the quiz, he frowned. "Lucy, after your last grade, I don't know what you're grinning at. I'd like you to take this a little more seriously."

"Don't worry," said Lucy. "I'm going to do better on this one."

"Don't count your chickens before they hatch," warned Mr. Vega. "That's an old scientific formula."

He went down the row and continued to hand out the papers.

"Why did you have to brag like that?" Dustin asked in a whisper.

"I don't know. He made me mad — just assuming that I'd do badly again," Lucy whispered.

"Dustin, Lucy, I want quiet," snapped Mr. Vega. "This is a test, not a social hour. All right, class, you can turn over the quiz."

Lucy looked at the test. It was a multiple-choice exam.

Lucy looked at the first question:

If M equals mass, weight affects the swing of a pendulum, and P represents momentum, the following formula is true.

A) $1 - M = pv + mm$
B) $p = MV$
C) $PE = mgh$
D) $p = mm^2$

Seeing the formulas with no words brought up the familiar panicky feeling in Lucy. But she took a deep breath.

On the swing, she had gone the same number of swings — the momentum — but the speed was cut by her weight.

She marked B.

Then she went down to the next question.

She took another deep breath and let it out, remembering that Mr. Vega had said that a brain needs oxygen. She answered all the questions. Her neck was getting stiff from the tension. She rubbed it and felt a knot. She twisted her neck back and forth.

"Keep your eyes to yourself, please," warned Mr. Vega.

Lucy turned beet red.

She was so startled that she dropped her pencil.

She bent down to pick it up and when she did, she saw Albert draw a piece of paper from his sock and hand it to Joey.

Neither of them saw her. Lucy sat up.

She tried to check her answers, but her mind wouldn't work. All she could think of was that Joey and Albert were cheating. They had made such a big deal out of her cheating at bowling, making her feel like an outcast, worse than any outlaw.

Mr. Vega collected the exams.

The bell rang.

Lucy walked out in a daze.

"That was a hard one," said Melanie. "It was stuff I had studied, but I forgot the details."

"I know I did okay," said Joey with a grin.

"That's the first one that I could relax about. Thanks, Melanie."

"Yeah, we aced that one," said Albert.

"Melanie, the Pacers are having an exhibition game this weekend," said Joey. "Albert's coming, and we'll sit in my father's box. Do you want to go?"

Melanie looked at Lucy as if for permission. Lucy was glaring at Joey.

"Uh, I can't," stammered Melanie. "Thanks."

Albert and Joey walked down the hall laughing.

"Say, Melanie?" asked Dustin, interrupting. "Did you catch that one question on momentum?"

"Dustin, shut up," snapped Melanie. She ran down the hall.

"What's wrong with her?" Dustin asked Lucy.

"I'm not sure," said Lucy.

"She acted like she's mad at me," said Dustin. "I didn't do anything wrong."

"Maybe she's mad at me," said Lucy.

"Why should she be mad at you? She's the one who stole your boyfriend."

"He wasn't my boyfriend," said Lucy. "And Melanie's my best friend, or at least *was* my best friend. I'm not sure what we are now. It's just . . ."

"What?" asked Dustin.

Lucy bit her lip. She didn't know what to do. Lucy hated tattlers.

"You gotta promise me not to tell anyone," Lucy said to Dustin.

"Cross my heart and hope to die," teased Dustin.

"This isn't funny, Dustin," said Lucy. "I mean it. If I tell you something, you gotta promise me that you absolutely won't tell a soul."

"Okay, whatever you tell me, I promise not to tell a living person. Do you want me to promise not to tell a dead person either?" he asked.

"Nobody — no kid or adult."

"What is it?" asked Dustin.

"I think Joey and Albert cheated, and Melanie helped them," whispered Lucy.

Lucy had thought she had seen everything, but the very last thing she had expected was to see Dustin explode in anger.

He flung his books to the floor. The sound was like a gunshot.

Mr. Vega came out of his room. "What was that?" he demanded.

"Nothing," said Lucy, "Dustin dropped his books."

Lucy was ready to pull Dustin away if he looked like he might say something.

"Well, try to keep the noise down in the hall. Don't you two have another class?"

"We have study hall," said Lucy quickly. "We're going."

Dustin picked up his books. He hugged them to his chest.

"You shouldn't have thrown your books," Lucy said to him.

Dustin's lips were in a tight line. "I hate cheaters," he said.

Lucy stared at him. "You're standing with one," she reminded him. "You've been studying with one."

Dustin shook his head. "That was different. That was just a stupid bowling game, and you only did it to impress Joey. It didn't make any difference."

"I don't see how this is really different," said Lucy, still feeling a little shocked by the strength of Dustin's reaction.

"Yeah, well, this *affects* me!" said Dustin. "What's the point of studying if everybody can cheat? It skews the whole grading system. Mr. Vega is one of the toughest teachers in the school. If I get a good grade from him, it counts. But if Joey and Albert can get a good grade from cheating, what's the point?"

"But that's exactly how Joey and Albert felt

when I cheated on bowling," argued Lucy. "They just cared about that more than you did. This is the same thing."

"That's a stupid argument," said Dustin. He stalked off.

Lucy ran after him. "Remember, you promised not to tell anybody," she reminded him.

"All you care about is saving Joey's skin," shouted Dustin.

"I do not," Lucy protested, but she was talking to Dustin's back.

23

Mr. Vega waited a week to hand back the exams. He placed them on the students' desks face down. Lucy snuck a look at her grade. Her mouth dropped open.

Dustin glanced over at her.

"I got an A," Lucy whispered excitedly.

Dustin looked at his grade. He frowned. "What's wrong?" Lucy whispered.

"I got a B," said Dustin.

Lucy felt a little bit badly that Dustin hadn't done as well, but her competitive juices were running. If she could get a better grade than Dustin on one test, who knew what she could do?

Maybe she'd go into science after all — be a doctor — be the one who finds a cure for AIDS, win the Nobel Prize. Lucy could see her parents, who would be so proud of her at the award ceremony.

"Lucy Lovello, Joey Rich, and Albert Barber, I'd like to see you after class," said Mr. Vega when he finished handing back the papers.

Lucy snapped out of her daydream. She glanced at Joey. He was chewing his thumbnail anxiously. Why would Mr. Vega want to see the three of them?

Mr. Vega looked at a calendar on his desk. "Oh, I forgot. I have a meeting with the principal right after class. Can you meet me immediately after school?"

"I have basketball practice with you," said Lucy.

"This is far more important," said Mr. Vega.

Lucy swallowed hard.

Lucy barely heard his lecture on population mathematics and ecology during the rest of the class. She was too worried about what Mr. Vega could possibly see as the connection between her and Albert and Joey.

Whatever it was, it wasn't good.

As soon as the bell rang, she stood at the door and waited for Joey and Albert. They were whispering together.

"What grade did you get?" Lucy asked them.

"A," said Albert.

"Me, too," said Joey. "It's the first A I got in this school."

"Yeah, and I know how you got it," said Lucy bitterly.

"What does that mean?" snapped Albert.

"I saw you guys cheat," whispered Lucy.

"What's going on?" asked Melanie. She sounded worried.

"I just know Mr. Vega doesn't want to congratulate us on our grades," said Lucy. "What did you get, Melanie?"

"I only got a B plus," said Melanie.

"What are you giving us dirty looks for?" asked Albert defensively, misinterpreting Lucy's worried look for a dirty one. "We didn't have anything to do with your grade. Come on, Joey. This girl has turned out to be a goofball and a cheater. Leave her alone."

Albert pulled on Joey's arm. Joey looked back at Lucy. "Relax," he said. "Mr. Vega can't prove anything. Just keep quiet and nothing will go wrong."

Joey took off down the hall.

"I can't believe this is happening to me," wailed Lucy.

"What are you so worried about?" Melanie asked. "You got an A. I got a B plus."

"Yeah, but Mr. Vega thinks that I cheated to get it," said Lucy.

"You don't know that," said Melanie.

"What do you want to bet on the probability?" asked Lucy bitterly.

"You didn't cheat, did you?" Melanie asked.

Lucy gave Melanie a dirty look. "No. I didn't. But Joey and Albert did. Doesn't it bother you at all that Joey got a better grade than you did and he cheated?"

Melanie took a deep breath. "Yeah," she admitted. "But Joey and Albert were scared stiff they were going to flunk the next pop quiz. They just didn't know when it would be."

"So you told them I thought the quiz was going to be on Friday and they cheated," said Lucy.

"They wanted help thinking of a place to hide the answers. I couldn't think of any place that wasn't obvious."

"Neither could they," said Lucy. "I saw them pull it out of their socks. It stinks."

"Their socks?" asked Melanie. "Their socks stink?"

"No, cheating. It really stinks."

"You did it on the bowling score. Lots of kids cheat," said Melanie.

"I did it once, and it was stupid. I just wanted

to impress Joey, and he wasn't worth it."

Melanie didn't say anything.

"He isn't, Melanie," said Lucy.

Melanie still didn't answer.

"I bet you got a low grade because you were upset that you helped them. I know you, Melanie. You love science. You must have been nervous because you thought Joey and Albert might cheat. That's why you wouldn't go to the game with him."

Melanie sighed. "B plus is not a low grade."

"It is for you," said Lucy. "Why didn't you go out on a date with Joey?"

"I didn't go with him because I was worried it would hurt you, if you really want to know. But if he asks me again, I'll go — even though I don't even like basketball too much."

"I don't think you'll enjoy a date with a cheater."

"You're just jealous because he likes me more than he likes you," said Melanie.

Lucy shook her head. "Wrong. Dead wrong."

"Lucy, you're acting like a child. We're supposed to be grown up now."

"Does grown up mean excusing Joey when he cheats?" asked Lucy.

"You wanted me to excuse you when you

cheated," said Melanie. "You're the one who everybody thinks is a cheater."

"Do you think that?" Lucy asked Melanie.

Melanie wouldn't look at her. She walked away. Lucy grabbed her. "I didn't cheat on that quiz. I swear it."

"It's not me you have to convince, it's Mr. Vega. And in case you didn't notice, I'm not the one who got called in for cheating."

"Yeah, but you helped Joey and Albert. That's just as bad."

"Well, I seem to be surrounded by cheaters, don't I?" said Melanie.

Lucy watched her go. Great, thought Lucy. I've got a reputation as a cheater, a teacher who's sure that I've cheated, and on top of that, I've lost my best friend. Junior high is not my idea of a good time.

24

At the end of the school day, Lucy made her way back to Mr. Vega's room. She stood uneasily in the doorway. Albert was already in the room. His feet stuck out into the aisle. Mr. Vega stood by his desk, looking at papers.

Joey touched her shoulder. Lucy jumped.

"You scared me," she said.

"I guess it's time to go in and face the music," he said.

"How come you and Albert didn't go in to-gether?" Lucy asked.

"Albert thought it would be smarter if we went in separately," said Joey. "He's good at thinking like that."

Lucy shook her head. She started to go into the room. Joey fidgeted with his books. "Look, Lucy, I'm sorry you got mixed up in this. This wasn't your fault. But please, please, don't tell on us."

Joey's eyes were genuinely pleading.

"I'm not a snitch," said Lucy. She walked into the classroom.

Mr. Vega looked up. "Ah, there you are, Ms. Lovello and Mr. Rich. Have you finished your conference in the hall?"

Lucy's heart sank. If Mr. Vega was starting out sarcastically, there was no hope.

Albert gave Joey a little smile.

Mr. Vega sat on the edge of his desk. His left leg dangled and moved up and down nervously. "The very toughest job that I've found as a teacher is to have to accuse a student of cheating," he said. He looked at all three of them.

"But when three students on the same day pull their grades up from flunking to an A — and answer the questions in the exact same way, I have to act. You all missed only one question, and it was the same question."

"Wouldn't chaos theory explain the unexplainable?" blurted out Lucy. "Because random events *do* happen."

Albert gave her a dirty look, but Lucy felt that her question was legitimate.

"Yes, Lucy, mathematical theory would explain it, but as good scientists, we'll have to see if we can repeat the experiment."

"I don't think you should treat your students as an experiment," mumbled Lucy.

Albert raised his hand. Mr. Vega nodded. "Yes, Albert."

"Mr. Vega, Joey and I studied harder than we ever have before. I don't know about Lucy. But I know that you convinced Joey and me that the only way to get good grades from you was to study hard."

Albert lied so easily. Joey at least looked a little uncomfortable.

"That's fine, Albert," said Mr. Vega dryly. "But I think I will take Lucy's approach."

Joey looked at Lucy suspiciously, as if she had somehow sneaked behind his back and told on him.

"What's that?" asked Joey. "Lucy's no different from us. Just 'cause she's a girl — if we're in trouble, she should be, too."

"I was talking about her reference to things I've said in class," said Mr. Vega. "We will try to repeat the experiment. You will come here before first period Monday. And I will give you a *test*. This test will cover not just the current material, but everything we have studied so far."

"That's fair," said Albert.

Lucy swiveled her head. It wasn't fair. It was much harder than any of the pop quizzes because quizzes only had a few questions. Tests were longer — and harder.

Albert looked so smug. Lucy just knew that he had a plan to cheat again and that Joey would go along with it.

"That's all," said Mr. Vega. "Lucy, perhaps you'd like to skip basketball practice this afternoon in order to study."

Lucy felt those were the final words of doom. Mr. Vega was sure that she had cheated. He was probably ready to cut her from the team because her grades were so low. He might as well have said that she needn't ever go to basketball practice again.

"I'll see the three of you Monday morning. Good luck," said Mr. Vega.

Lucy raised her hand. "What happens if we get a lower score on the test Monday? Does that mean that you'll think we cheated? It could have been just a lucky break — like the butterfly wings."

"Lucy, your job is to study — this was a warning. I have no proof that any of you cheated. That's why I'm giving you all a second chance."

"Stop gibbering," whispered Albert. "You'll only make it worse."

Dustin and Melanie were waiting for them when they came out. "What happened?" Dustin asked.

"He thinks we all cheated. We have to take a test on Monday," said Lucy. "On everything from the beginning of the semester. I'll flunk it."

"We won't," said Albert, patting his pants leg.

Lucy pushed him hard in the chest. "Don't you dare cheat on Monday!" she said.

"You don't tell me what to do, Lucy," said Albert.

"You can't cheat again. It'll get us all in trouble."

"What we do isn't your business," said Albert. "Right, Joey?"

Joey nodded.

"Besides," sneered Albert, "you cheat by studying with Dustin and getting the answers from him."

"I don't just hide the answers and take them into the test," said Lucy.

"It's cheating, cheater," said Albert. "You cheated at your best friend's birthday party — that's much worse than what we did."

"He's kind of right, Lucy," said Joey. "I'm not cheating. I'm just surviving. You didn't *need* to cheat on bowling."

"You're just afraid to bring home a bad grade

to your dad," argued Lucy. "But he can't fire you the way he does some coach who doesn't win."

"Leave my dad out of this," snapped Joey. He was getting mad. It was the first real emotion Joey had shown since the whole ordeal with Mr. Vega began.

"Joey doesn't need pop psychology from you," said Albert. He laughed. "Get it? It was a joke. 'Pop' psychology — about Joey's pop?"

Melanie gave Lucy a helpless look. "What's the big deal? I mean, you *do* study with Dustin."

"Yeah," said Joey eagerly. "It's like Albert said, that's kind of like cheating."

Melanie, Joey, and Albert walked away — together.

Lucy was left alone in the hall.

Mr. Vega came out of his room. "Lucy?" he asked. "Were you waiting for me?"

Lucy felt herself near tears. She shook her head.

"I'm not trying to punish you," said Mr. Vega.

"But you are," Lucy said. She sighed. "I've got one question," she said. She paused. "Well, maybe it's kind of a confession. Dustin and I study together for your quizzes. Is that cheating?"

"I don't consider that cheating," said Mr. Vega. "Look, scientists work together all the time.

They're always bouncing ideas off one another, working together, gossiping together, that's how breakthroughs happen."

"Dustin and I figured out a pattern to when you give tests," said Lucy.

Mr. Vega's eyes gleamed. "That's very smart of you."

"But you accused me of cheating," protested Lucy.

"I suspected you — that's different. If studying's what the three of you did, I'm pleased. You should do well on Monday's test. But I have no way of knowing if you're telling the truth or if you're lying and really cheated."

Lucy hated — hated — the fact that Mr. Vega might think she was lying.

"I'm not a liar," she said defiantly.

"Lucy, just study hard over the weekend, and you can prove it to me."

"But if I don't do well on the test, then you'll think I am a cheater and I'll never be able to prove it to you."

"We'll cross that bridge when we come to it," said Mr. Vega.

Lucy hated it when teachers used the word "we." It was Lucy who had to pass or fail, not Mr. Vega.

25

Lucy knew that she would have to study all weekend. She spent all day Saturday holed up in her room. She took out all her notes and spread them on her desk. She took out the earlier pop quizzes and tried to memorize which answers she had gotten wrong.

She was getting a headache. Her English and social studies homework would have to slide.

Her mother knocked on her door. "I've never seen you study so hard," she said. "Dinner will be ready in a few minutes. Will you help me make the salad?"

"I don't have time," Lucy grumbled. Then she tried to take a deep breath. "Sorry, Mom. I've got a really big science test on Monday. Would it be okay if I eat dinner in my room and skip helping — just for tonight?"

"How come you're not studying with Dustin?" asked her mother.

"Dustin doesn't have to take this test," said Lucy. "It's just Joey Rich, Albert Barber, and me."

Her mother sat down on the edge of the bed. "That sounds strange. Why do the three of you have extra work? And what ever happened between you and Joey? You were so excited to go out with him."

"Joey Rich is a liar and a cheat," said Lucy. "And if you want to know what I have in common with him — it's that everybody thinks I'm a liar and a cheat, too, including Mr. Vega. There, now are you happy that I'm in such good company?"

Mrs. Lovello stood up. "Who says you're a liar and a cheat?" snapped her mother. She looked like she was ready to defend her daughter against all comers.

"Mom," said Lucy, "you can't help me with this."

"Lucy, you are *not* a liar or a cheat, and I will not have anyone saying those things about you."

"I cheated at Melanie's bowling party. That's why Joey broke up with me."

"You cheated at *bowling*?" her mother exclaimed. "Is that what this is about?"

"No," said Lucy. "It's much more complicated than that. But, yeah, that's what it started out with."

"Lucy, did you cheat on your exam?"

"Mr. Vega thinks I did," said Lucy.

"But did you?" asked Lucy's mother.

"No," said Lucy.

"Then that's that," said her mother. "If you want to keep studying, I'll bring you some dinner."

"So you believe me?" asked Lucy, feeling astonished.

"That you want dinner up here?" asked her mother.

"No, Mom," said Lucy. "Do you believe me that I didn't cheat on my exam?"

"Yes," said Lucy's mother.

"What about cheating at bowling?" asked Lucy.

"Lucy, you're the one who has to live with your mistakes — all you can do is try to learn from them. I know that sounds like a stupid cliché from one of my columns, but that's the best I can do for you."

"It's not bad," said Lucy softly, "as advice columns go."

26

By Sunday night, Lucy felt like she had scientific formulas coming out of her ears. She talked her mother into letting her eat in her room again.

There was a knock on the door. "Just leave it, Mom. I'm in the middle of a problem," shouted Lucy. "I'll pick it up."

"It's me — Melanie," said Melanie.

Lucy opened her door. "I thought you were my mom with my dinner."

"You get it delivered?" asked Melanie.

"I haven't stopped studying," said Lucy. "I think maybe I overdid it. I'll probably flunk because I studied too much."

"I don't think that's a real problem," said Melanie.

Melanie looked around the room with the papers and books spread out on every available surface. "I'm impressed."

Lucy cleared off a space on her bed so that Melanie could sit down. "I haven't done anything else all weekend. I can't even remember what it's like to turn on a television."

"Lucy, it's only been two days," said Melanie.

Lucy gave her a dirty look. "How come you aren't helping Joey and Albert?"

"I was," said Melanie. "They wanted all my old tests. I thought that wasn't such a bad idea. I figure that Mr. Vega will pick questions from the old tests randomly, so if they studied the old tests, they could do well."

"That's what I'm doing," said Lucy. "Only I do think it's possible to study too much. All of the formulas are starting to sound the same to me."

"Do you want me to quiz you?" asked Melanie.

"Is that what you've been doing for Joey and Albert?" asked Lucy.

Melanie looked guilty.

"They're going to cheat again, aren't they?" said Lucy.

Melanie looked away.

"*Awwgggh!*" said Lucy, making a choking sound. She fell down in a heap on the floor. "I studied all weekend, and they're going to cheat!"

"Albert is putting the answers on Joey's computer and cutting them into strips to fit in the rib of their socks. This time they're being much more scientific than the last time when they just stuffed a scribbled note into their shoes. They're even making sure the socks match the print. They are cheating. I thought I should come over and tell you."

"Why? So I can be the one to tattle on them? I don't want to do that."

Melanie shrugged. "I know. I just didn't think it was fair."

"So do you think I should cheat, too?"

"You could," said Melanie. "If you want to. I made a copy of their computer printout for you. You can use it if you want."

Melanie pulled out a piece of paper and handed it to Lucy. "Here are all the answers. You'll just have to figure out a place to hide it. I wouldn't put it in your socks. You should do something different. I could help you. You and I are friends, aren't we? I hated having a fight with you."

"I hated having a fight with you," admitted Lucy.

"I want you to do as well as Joey and Albert. This proves I'm not boy crazy."

"Yeah, but I'm the one who has to cheat. You didn't cheat."

"I'm cheating by helping you."

"That's not what Mr. Vega says about studying together, except that I guess this isn't studying — this is outright cheating." Lucy folded the paper reluctantly. "I'm not sure I want it," she said.

"It'll just even the playing field for the three of you," said Melanie. "You'll all go into the test with the same advantage."

"Yeah," said Lucy bitterly. "We're all cheaters."

Melanie sighed. "Can we be friends again?"

"Because you're helping me cheat, too?" asked Lucy.

"Why are you being so mean to me?" Melanie demanded.

Lucy shook her head. "I'm not trying to be mean to you, Melanie. It seems like junior high is all about cheating and boys." Lucy waved the paper in the air.

"All you have to do is get by on this exam," said Melanie. "Then you don't have to worry about it. You can stop cheating after that."

"Are you gonna keep helping Joey and Albert cheat?" asked Lucy.

"I don't know," said Melanie. "They're getting better grades than I am."

"It isn't worth it," said Lucy.

"Yeah, tell that to me when Albert gets into any college he wants to, and I don't."

"Albert Barber is a jerk," said Lucy.

"Albert Barber is a guy who's probably gonna get what he wants," said Melanie.

"And what about Joey? Is *he* getting what he wants? Am I? Are you?"

"I don't know what you're talking about," said Melanie. "I came over here to help you."

"I know, Melanie," said Lucy. "But if that's true, why do we both feel rotten?"

"I don't feel rotten," said Melanie defiantly.

Lucy looked at her. "This is me, remember? Lucy? The one who gave you the special crystal?"

"Who picked that out? You or Joey?" asked Melanie.

"How could you even ask me that? It was *my* present. Joey just asked me to sign his name to it."

"I feel rotten," admitted Melanie.

"So do I," confessed Lucy.

27

Lucy didn't throw away the paper that Melanie gave her. All night, whenever she took a break from studying, she played with it, folding and unfolding it.

When she woke up the next morning, she put on a long-sleeved rugby shirt with wide stripes. She experimented with slipping the folded-up paper in the ribs of the cuff of her shirt. The stripes disguised the paper, and it was very easy to slip out the paper and glance at it. Lucy practiced cheating with it. Then she went down for breakfast.

Her father brought her a glass of orange juice. "Mom said you've got a special science test today," said her dad. "She said you were studying like a demon."

Lucy looked at her mother. "Why would demons have to study?" asked Lucy. "You'd think if anybody would cheat, it would be a demon."

"At least you haven't lost your sense of humor," said her father. "Good luck today."

"You're *not* a cheater," Lucy's mother whispered and smiled.

Lucy touched the piece of paper tucked into her shirt.

She didn't talk to anybody on the school bus. She sat next to the window and stared out. When she arrived at school she went straight to Mr. Vega's room.

Joey and Albert were already there, standing outside of Mr. Vega's locked room.

"He's not here yet," said Albert. "Maybe he forgot."

"Fat chance," said Joey. He fidgeted with his socks. Lucy stared at him.

Lucy took the piece of paper from her sleeve. "Melanie came over last night. She told me what you guys were planning on doing. She gave me a copy, too."

"Hey," hissed Joey. "Be careful of that. Mr. Vega could come around the corner any moment. And don't be stupid in the exam. With just the three of us, Mr. Vega is going to be eagle-eyed." Joey leaned forward. "We aren't even using paper," he whispered. "We've got it on transparent acetate."

"Will you shut up?" said Albert. "You shouldn't be telling her *anything*."

Lucy looked at the paper in her hand. She crumpled it up and tore it into little pieces.

"Take off your socks," she said to Joey and Albert.

Joey and Albert laughed at her.

"Come on," she said. "Quickly."

"You are out of your mind," said Albert.

Lucy ignored him. "I'm not kidding. It's gone too far. Don't do it."

"Lucy, you do what you want," said Joey. "I'm not flunking this test."

"Joey, this is only junior high science. Are you both going to cheat your way through high school and college? Do you want to go into every exam like this?"

"It's Mr. Vega's fault. He just gets off on being a tough grader," argued Joey.

"Right," said Lucy. "And it was your fault that I cheated at bowling because I knew you and your dad liked winners."

Joey stared at her. "Is that why you cheated?"

Lucy nodded. "Pretty dumb excuse, isn't it? And so is your excuse. There'll always be a dumb excuse. Take off your socks, or I'll tell Mr. Vega that you're cheating."

"You wouldn't do that," said Joey.

"Try me," said Lucy.

Joey wouldn't meet Lucy's eyes. "Forget her," said Albert. "She's a dork and a cheater."

Joey leaned down. He took off his shoes and peeled off his socks.

Lucy's breath was shallow. She couldn't believe that Joey was following her orders.

Just then Mr. Vega came around the corner.

"What's going on here?" he demanded. "Joey, do you have a hot foot?"

Joey looked at Lucy. "Uh, no," he stammered. "Well, uh — it's a superstition. I always do better on exams without socks. Is that okay?"

Mr. Vega shook his head. "It doesn't bother me if it doesn't bother you," he said. "Come on in."

"Uh, Albert," said Joey. "Isn't it good luck for you to take off your socks?"

"No," said Albert evenly, "it isn't." Albert defiantly pushed his way into the room. He took a seat.

Mr. Vega pulled out the test papers and handed them out.

Lucy looked at the questions. Mr. Vega *had* taken questions from each of the pop quizzes. Lucy tried to remember the right answers. Her hands felt sweaty.

Mr. Vega tapped his pencil. He patrolled up and down the aisles.

Albert sat like a pretzel in his chair with his right leg tucked under him the way he always did. But when Mr. Vega was up in front of the room, Lucy caught Albert rolling down his socks and then quickly writing down an answer.

Mr. Vega didn't catch it.

Finally, Mr. Vega turned. "That's all the time you have," he said. "Pass the tests to the front."

Albert got up to leave.

"Stay right where you are, Mr. Barber. You, too, Lucy and Joey. It was a multiple-choice exam, and since I know you're all as anxious as I am to see how you did, I'll grade them right here."

"I'm not that anxious," said Albert quickly.

"Neither am I," said Joey.

"Sit down, all of you," said Mr. Vega.

He took out a red pencil and quickly graded the exams.

"Lucy and Joey," he said. "You both passed. Joey you got a D plus, Lucy a B plus. Lucy, good work. Joey, I'd like you to try to pull your grades up."

"What about me?" demanded Albert.

"Albert, you got an A," said Mr. Vega. Albert

sat there with a smirk on his face.

"That's why I prepared some oral questions that I was planning to ask anybody who repeated their A. Lucy and Joey, you can go."

"That's not fair!" protested Albert. "You're punishing me for getting a good grade."

"It's not punishment," said Mr. Vega dryly. "Just think of it as a chance to show off. You like to show off, don't you?"

Joey was staring at Albert. "Mr. Rich," said Mr. Vega, "I said you can leave. It is still the beginning of the school year. Lucy knows that I have never believed that the only thing that counts in a basketball game is the final two minutes. You have all year to study — as will Mr. Barber. All three of you have a lifetime of studying in front of you."

Mr. Vega got up and shepherded them out the door. He closed the door firmly, leaving just Albert and himself inside. Lucy wouldn't have changed places with Albert for anything.

Joey let out a deep sigh. "I think he knows Albert and I cheated on the last quiz," said Joey. "What do you think?"

"I think that comment about the final two minutes says it all," said Lucy. "He's going to be on us all year."

"What do you think he's going to do to Albert?"

Joey asked. He paced outside the room.

"I don't know," said Lucy.

"Thanks," said Joey.

"For what?" asked Lucy.

"If you hadn't made me take off my socks, I would have cheated, and both Albert and I would have been locked behind the door."

Lucy wondered why that realization didn't make her feel better. She had saved Joey's skin, and she hadn't cheated.

But she was still scared. Maybe because she knew that the line between being on one side of the door or on the other was pretty slippery.

28

Joey put his ear to the door to Mr. Vega's room. "It's awfully quiet in there," he said.

Lucy looked at her watch. "He's had Albert in there alone for twenty minutes. The bell's going to ring any minute now. Maybe we should go."

"I don't think I should leave Albert alone," said Joey.

Dustin, Melanie, and Spider came down the hall. "What happened?" asked Melanie.

"Lucy and I passed, well, I did just barely," said Joey.

"How come you're not wearing any socks?" Dustin asked. "It's about forty degrees out."

"Ask Lucy," said Joey. "She's the one with all the answers."

"I got a B plus," said Lucy.

"Not bad," said Dustin. "I guess studying by yourself paid off."

"I liked studying together better. I talked to Mr. Vega. He doesn't think studying together is cheating. In fact, he says it's how scientific breakthroughs are made. And he kind of hinted we might be right about that quiz-pattern stuff."

Just then the door opened and Albert barreled out of Mr. Vega's door looking furious. He grabbed Joey. "Come on," he said. "We're gonna go to your father. I'm gonna get that dude fired. He asked me questions *nobody* would have known — and then he gave me an F. Your father's on the school board. He can get rid of Mr. Vega."

Joey drew back. "I'm not going to my father and getting Mr. Vega fired."

"Why not?" insisted Albert. "You said your dad would be on our side."

Joey shook his head. "I'm not going to my dad," he said firmly.

"Oh, man," complained Albert. "Are you going to tell your dad you got a D minus?"

Joey shrugged. "It was a D plus."

Albert loped down the hall, hitting each locker as he went. The clanks echoed through the hall. Spider watched him go.

Lucy looked at Joey.

"Albert's kind of a jerk," said Spider.

Lucy started to laugh. Melanie giggled.

"What's so funny?" Joey asked.

"Nothing, really," said Lucy. "None of this was funny — and, yes, Spider, Albert *is* kind of a jerk!"

"It's over," said Joey. "You passed. And Mr. Vega doesn't think you cheated."

"He doesn't think you cheated, either," said Lucy.

"Right," said Joey. "He just gave me a D."

"A D plus," said Lucy.

Joey made a face.

"You could study with Dustin and me," said Lucy. "We could make a study group."

"What about me?" asked Melanie.

"Dustin thought you were too smart to want to study with the rest of us."

Melanie punched Dustin lightly on the arm. "That was stupid," she said. "I like to be challenged. Lucy's always been a challenge."

"What about me?" asked Spider.

"Is it for couples?" Joey asked.

"No way," said Lucy and Melanie in unison. Lucy put her arm though Melanie's. "I didn't use the paper you gave me," she whispered.

"I didn't think you would," said Melanie.

"Is that why you want to study with us?" Lucy asked her. "Because I didn't cheat?"

Melanie shook her head. "No," she said. "I still think Joey's kind of cute."

Lucy looked over at Joey. "He is, kind of," she admitted.

"Does this mean we both like the same boy?" Melanie asked her.

"Please," she said. "Let's not complicate things any more than they are already."

"Okay," said Melanie. "I'll stick with Dustin. He is smart."

"I thought we said this wasn't for couples," whispered Lucy.

"We are in junior high," said Melanie. "A science study group sounds so nerdy."

"It's better than flunking science," whispered Lucy back.

"What are you two whispering about?" Joey asked.

"Nothing," said Lucy and Melanie together. Lucy and Melanie separated and Melanie started down the hall.

Lucy fell into step with Joey.

"There's one question I've got to ask," she said. "Why did you take off your socks for me? I really didn't think you would."

"I thought you'd really tell on me if I didn't," said Joey.

"I wouldn't have," said Lucy. "You know, I never understood. Why did you ask me out in the first place?"

"I thought you were funny and smart," said Joey.

"Oh," said Lucy. "Melanie's the smart one."

"Yeah, but you're the funny one. Why did you cheat at bowling?" Joey asked.

"I thought it would make you like me," said Lucy.

"That's pretty dumb," said Joey.

"I know," admitted Lucy. "I was tempted to cheat on this exam, too."

"Tell me about it," said Joey.

"I didn't think you were going to take your socks off," said Lucy.

"I liked you before you cheated," said Joey.

"I liked myself that way, too," said Lucy.

"What about now?" Joey asked.

"Now isn't so bad," Lucy smiled.

About the Author

Elizabeth Levy is the author of over fifty books for children and teenagers. Among her many novels are *The Computer That Said Steal Me*, *A Different Twist*, and THE GYMNASTS series. She is well known for the humor in her stories, even when the subject is scary, as in the SOMETHING QUEER mysteries. Although she knows that cheating isn't funny, she believes that learning to laugh and forgive your mistakes is the only way to go forward.

Ms. Levy now lives in New York City.

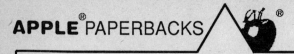

APPLE® PAPERBACKS

Pick an Apple and Polish Off Some Great Reading!

BEST-SELLING APPLE TITLES

❏ MT43944-8 **Afternoon of the Elves** Janet Taylor Lisle   **$2.75**

❏ MT43109-9 **Boys Are Yucko** Anna Grossnickle Hines   **$2.95**

❏ MT43473-X **The Broccoli Tapes** Jan Slepian   **$2.95**

❏ MT40961-1 **Chocolate Covered Ants** Stephen Manes   **$2.95**

❏ MT45436-6 **Cousins** Virginia Hamilton   **$2.95**

❏ MT44036-5 **George Washington's Socks** Elvira Woodruff   **$2.95**

❏ MT45244-4 **Ghost Cadet** Elaine Marie Alphin   **$2.95**

❏ MT44351-8 **Help! I'm a Prisoner in the Library** Eth Clifford   **$2.95**

❏ MT43618-X **Me and Katie (The Pest)** Ann M. Martin   **$2.95**

❏ MT43030-0 **Shoebag** Mary James   **$2.95**

❏ MT46075-7 **Sixth Grade Secrets** Louis Sachar   **$2.95**

❏ MT42882-9 **Sixth Grade Sleepover** Eve Bunting   **$2.95**

❏ MT41732-0 **Too Many Murphys** Colleen O'Shaughnessy McKenna   **$2.95**

Available wherever you buy books, or use this order form.

- -

Scholastic Inc., P.O. Box 7502, 2931 East McCarty Street, Jefferson City, MO 65102

Please send me the books I have checked above. I am enclosing $_____ (please add $2.00 to cover shipping and handling). Send check or money order — no cash or C.O.D.s please.

Name_____ **Birthdate**_____

Address _____

City_____ **State/Zip** _____

Please allow four to six weeks for delivery. Offer good in the U.S.A. only. Sorry, mail orders are not available to residents of Canada. Prices subject to change.

APP693